A WITCH, HER CAT AND A PIRATE
A tale of a Scarborough Witch, her Cat,
John Paul Jones and the Battle of
Flamborough.

By Graham A. Rhodes

First published 2016
Revised 2022

Templar Publishing Scarborough N. Yorkshire

Also available in the series Agnes the Scarborough Witch -

A Witch, Her Cat and the Ship Wreckers.

A Witch, Her Cat and the Devil Dogs.

A Witch, Her Cat and a Viking Hoard (in preparation)

Dedication

This is the first book of Agnes. It would have been impossible without the help and encouragement of the following people –

Yvonne, Jesse, Frankie & Heather (& Granddad), Richard, The Badgers Of Bohemia, Tubbs & Missy, Magenta, Anna (Whose gig at the SJT Started all this off) & all at Cellars, Dennis & Dave, & Ysanne (RIP).

Many of the streets and places mentioned in this book still exist in Scarborough's old town and up on the moors. They are well worth visiting. Once again I have taken the liberty of using the names of old Scarborough fishing families. I hope they don't mind their ancestors appearing here. However the names and characters are all fictitious and should not be confused with anyone living or dead.

List of Characters

Agnes 21st & 18th Centuries

Our hero, an elderly lady who, as far as she knows, is over three hundred years old. She has no memory of who she is or where she came from. She lives in the same cottage in the Old Town of Scarborough in both centuries. She is either a wize woman or a witch, depending on who is telling the story. She is also a rather excellent computer hacker.

Marmaduke 21st & 18th Centuries

Marmaduke lives with Agnes in her cottage. In the twenty first he is an old, grumpy, one eared, one eyed, sardine addicted cat. In the 18th century he is a one eyed one eared six foot high ex-highwayman with very dangerous habits.

Andrew Marks 18th Century

The proprietor of the Chandlery situated on Scarborough's 18th century harbour side. Andrew is the eyes and ears of the small port. Nothing comes or goes in or out the port without him knowing about it, either legal or illegal.

The Garrison Commander 18th Century

The military commander of the Garrison based at Scarborough's Castle. Posted to Scarborough for a mistake he made during the American of Independence he is very definitely a soldier of the old school.

Lieutenant Smalls
A young military man and the right hand man of the Garrison Commander. An intelligent and thoughtful officer who could go far.

Whitby John
Ex-fisherman and landlord of The Three Mariners, Agnes favourite public house.

Salmon Martin
A fisherman and regular of the Three Mariners.

Sammy Storr
A dead fisherman.

John Paul Jones
Either a pirate or the founder of the American Navy, depending on which history book you read.

An Indian Shaman.
A Red Indian supporter of American Independence.

Machinitou
A great evil.

A WITCH, HER CAT AND A PIRATE
A tale of a Scarborough Witch, her Cat, John Paul Jones and the Battle of Flamborough.

By Graham A. Rhodes

Chapter One

The warm September sun blazed down from a clear blue sky, its light sparkled from the tops of the incoming waves, danced among the masts of the boats bobbing lazily in the harbour and reflected among the red roofs and whitewashed yards of the old town houses that sought shade under the shadow of the old castle on the cliff top. It eventually came to rest on the ginger fur of a large, one eyed cat, sleeping on the top of a green wheelie-bin standing in a whitewashed yard. The yard held pots of herbs and flowers whose blossoms created splashes of colour in the glaring white heat. The yard was situated at the back of an old house. All the houses in this part of the old town were old. That's why it was called the Old Town. Some had been build way back in 1712, almost three hundred years ago.

Everyone who walked down the street could tell how old the house was because a small wooden plaque was nailed to the wall. It said "Built in 1712", so it must be true. Agnes knew, she should know - she lived there, she was the owner of the house. She had owned it for many, many years now. In fact Agnes could remember when the house was first built. She was its first and only owner. She had been "given" it by a grateful sea captain whom she had helped when no one else would or, for that matter, could.

It had proved to be a very awkward experience for both of them. For the sea captain because to lose ones ship when it was moored in the harbour wasn't very good for his reputation, and for Agnes because it meant that she had been forced to reveal to the Captain the fact she was a witch, and, as she lived in a very small town, very soon everyone else knew she was a witch.

As a result of their actions the sea captain had decided that discretion would save him from an awful lot of trouble. He slipped out of the country just before the H.M. Customs Officers knocked down his front door. He never returned. Many years later Agnes learnt he'd been lost at sea when he was captaining a small ketch running from Dutch customs. The story claimed it had sunk during a particularly violent North Sea storm. Agnes had checked the story, and believed it. She then checked the deeds of the house; it was hers for as long as she wanted it. Three hundred years later she still hadn't found a better place to live.

Over the years people came and went, they lived and died, soon there was only a distant memory of a witch who helped a sea captain, a memory that became a legend helped by a bright young musician who wrote a ballad about it. It was still sung today where people, armed with glasses of real ale, gathered to sing traditional songs. Agnes had even heard it once on a record sung by a folk group who played electric instruments, however the people with the glasses of real ale looked down at their noses at such performances and claimed it wasn't traditional. Agnes tended to agree with them, but for different reasons – over the years the lyrics to the song had changed. For some reason the witch had changed into a mermaid and the sea captain, instead of being an grumpy middle aged man with one leg who would skin you alive as soon as look at you, was now a handsome young man dragged away from his lady-love who was left to walk the salt sea strand. Agnes knew what the salt sea strand was, but she doubted that the people who sung such words, with or without glasses of real ale, either didn't know or didn't care.

Over the years the residents of the old town had come to know Agnes as a "wise woman", sometimes spelt "wize" just for the effect. According to tradition a wise woman is euphemism for a witch for people who are too polite to mention the "W" word, but it really just describes an old woman who dispenses wisdom like a doctor dispenses medicine. Although fault could be found with that analogy as Agnes also dispensed medicines, and knew a thing or two about herbs and curatives. For years people came to knock on her door, seeking cure-alls, advice and lost cats, but usually, whether they knew it or not, the only thing that the people who knocked on her door really needed was dose of common sense and a cup of tea. Agnes had endless quantities of both.

It was good sense that stopped Agnes from having her picture taken. She realised the need for that back at the turn of the last century when a photographer set up a portrait studio in the next street. When he was short of customers, which he frequently was, he would wander the streets with his huge wooden and brass camera attached to an even larger tripod. He would plant the tripod in the middle of the streets and take photographs that he claimed "would prove a valuable record" in the years to come. They had. Sometime in the 1970's when a student was doing some research on the buildings of the old town they searched through the long dead photographers pictures and noticed an uncanny resemblance to the old woman in the background of a picture taken in 1899 to the old woman who lived at the end of the street now. She even seemed to be wearing the same cloths – despite the fact that over seventy years had passed. In order to stop the story spreading Agnes carefully explained to the student that all old women looked the same, irrespective of the period. Then she smiled her special smile. The special smile worked, it always did, and the student agreed and went away wondering why she was looking at old photographs and bothering old women in the first place.

In the meanwhile Agnes had decided that enough was enough – she didn't need to go around explaining the impossibility of her featuring in old photographs taken a hundred years ago to inquisitive people. The last thing she need was people making connections or asking questions, so she opened the door to her cellar. Halfway down the staircase there was a bricked up doorway. Without even a pause she stepped through the bricks and simply disappeared. She reappeared almost instantly and walked back up the cellar steps to reappear inside her cottage at the end of the 19th century where she made very sure that her image didn't appear in any other photographs. The following morning a very puzzled photographer stood scratching his head, wondering how light had managed to leak into his glass plate negatives and fog them all, even those in the middle of the box where no light could possibly have leaked. He was still wondering as, once again he dragged his camera around the streets to retake them all. This time Agnes stayed indoors.

Back at the end of the 20th century Agnes sat down and created a special personal magic for her own use, only ·

she refused to call it magic, she created what she thought of as a special cloaking – whatever it was called, it was something that made her head slightly ache and the centre of her palm itch whenever a camera was pointed in her direction. It wasn't painful, "awakening herself to problems" was how she would have explained it, should she feel the need to explain it to anyone. But there wasn't anyone, just her one-eyed cat sat outside sunning itself on the large green wheelie bin at the bottom of the yard.

These days, that is the days at the end of the 20th century, Agnes very rarely went out – frail old ladies weren't meant to go out by themselves, especially to the local pub, especially not at those prices. If she fancied a night out she'd slip back to the 18th century and pop to the old local pub. Back then the landlord was more cheerful, the beer a lot cheaper and people didn't call social services when they saw an old lady staggering home by herself after few rum toddies.

As to shopping, well since the invention of the internet and credit cards, supermarkets delivered these days. Once a fortnight a van and driver would make the treacherous journey through the tight little streets, knock on her door and place her order in her entrance porch. The supermarket companies who operated such a service would have been very surprised to discover that, despite owning a computer, Agnes didn't have a credit card, or even a telephone to call them up. All the supermarket knew was that there was an order on their system that needed supplying and that the bill was always paid. Agnes thought it better that way – especially as she didn't have a bank account either, but there again, she didn't need one.

If Agnes needed ready cash all she had to do was slip back to some point in time – pick up a few household objects, and then slip back to the present and put them into an auction. At the local auctioneers she was better known as the queen of the car boot sales. The things that she turned up with were a constant source of amazement to them. One week it was a Penny Black, in mint condition. Another week she'd turned up with an antique pistol that she claimed had been used during the Civil War, when the nearby Castle had been besieged. Despite its shiny and almost unused appearance, expert examination proved it was what Agnes claimed it was. Once, in the hope of finding the source of her treasure the auctioneers hired a private detective to follow her. After a month of lurking outside her house he gave up. All he had discovered was that she never seemed to go out and that her yard was haunted by a very large ginger cat with very sharp claws and a very bad temper. It was whilst he was waiting in the casualty ward of the local hospital that the private detective decided he was in the wrong job.

Agnes had stopped wondering about time travel, after all when you've been doing something for over three hundred years you eventually get used to it – she didn't question it, or puzzle or fret about it, she just did it. She often thought the world would be a lot better place if people stopped worrying about the how's, whys and wherefores and just did things. She did reflect that time travel was a whole lot easier when you could travel back with your own house and all its possessions. There were rules though – for example modern technology never travelled back in time. Her television and electric kettle were firmly rooted in the 20th century. She had thought about this for a long time and come to the conclusion that it was a good thing. She shuddered what would happen to the world had she turned up at her local pub in the 18th century with her electric carving knife and electric kettle – for one thing it would have killed conversation, for another thing she would never have been able to find an electric plug. She did wonder about joining the 20th century and wearing more fashionable clothes. She even found herself wondering about using make-up. Maybe even trying a bit of that cosmetic surgery she'd read so much about. It seemed that all woman over a certain age tried it, face lifts, tummy tucks, all manner of snips and reshaping. After seeing what they had to put up with she decided against it. Magic could alter her appearance for a little while, but cosmetic surgery looked too painful and time consuming for her to bother. She had considering getting her teeth fixed. Ever since an unfortunate incident with a very hard nut that had removed her two front teeth she hadn't been able to whistle properly, but there again old wise women were meant to have a couple of missing teeth. It was expected. No in the world that Agnes inhabited everything had its time and its place – it was just that she was able to slip between them all.

Before she stepped through her front door she checked a large jar on a shelf alongside many more similar jars. Without looking she dipped her hand inside and pulled out a number of coins. It was the right currency for 1779, a lot of large pennies, and a George III half guinea, more than enough for a couple of drinks. She stepped through the door.

Outside dusk was bringing the September day to an end and night was drawing over the small town. It had been a hot day and the suns warmth still radiated from the surrounding stone-walls and tight, cobbled streets. The smell of smoked kippers drifted up from the harbour side buildings and mingled with the acrid smoke that curled up from the chimneys that drew the smoke from the many tiny back room fires from the surrounding houses and cottages.

As she walked to the corner and turned into Castlegate Agnes could hear the noises of the 18th century drifting from every open window and door. Children shouted and yelled. Seagulls screamed. A dog barked. A horse and cart was negotiating the steep hill. A man was shouting at his wife. A group of angry woman had gathered around the pair offering verbal advice and threats. They all looked up as Agnes came into view and the argument quickly stopped. They all nodded politely as she walked passed. As soon as she turned the corner the fracas started up again. She managed to stop herself from turning back.

Agnes turned along a narrow alleyway squeezed between the backs of old timber framed houses, where the windows and doors were open and people shouted conversations with their neighbours from the comfort of their own back rooms. A stray dog was skulking along sniffing, hopeful that the smell he was following would lead to food. A cat hid on an outhouse roof hoping that the dog wouldn't see it. Seagulls drifted overhead screaming at the two animals below. Agnes turned right at the head of the narrow Dog and Duck Lane where she descended a flight of steep steps that led, very conveniently for her, straight towards the front door of the Three Mariners Inn.

She paused as she stepped inside to allow her eyes to get used to the dim light created by a row of flickering oil lanterns around the inside of the walls. No matter what the time of day it was always dark inside the Mariners. The lamplight reflected, bounced and fought its way through the clouds of stale tobacco smoke to illuminate a few customers sat hunched over their drinks in small groups of twos and threes. A couple of weather beaten men looked up at the new arrival and nodded a brief acknowledgement. Agnes nodded back. By the time she reached the counter Whitby John, the barman had drawn a measure of beer in a small leather mug. Saying her thank you's, she gathered it up, dropped a couple of coins on the bar surface and walked slowly across to the fireplace glowing at the far end of the room. The men already sat there noticed her arrival and quickly stood up, indicating the chair nearest the fire. Agnes nodded and took the seat. Despite the warmth of the day the fire in the Three Mariners never went out and warm as it was, the chair nearest the fireplace had been Agnes's ever since anyone could remember. Local legend had it that if anyone dare remain in her chair whilst Agnes was in the hostelry they would, in a very short space of time, suffer some sort of loss. Agnes liked local legends, especially when they were about her. It did her reputation good and a local witch needs a good reputation – otherwise people just didn't offer the right amount of respect. Of course, the fact that the man who had refused to give up the seat had drowned by falling off his own boat whilst fishing in the bay gave the legend a solid basis – however the legend conveniently forgot to mention the fact that on that particular night there had been a severe storm in which only an idiot or a drunk would have taken a boat out. It turned out the unfortunate man was both.

Sometime after his body had been found washed ashore and buried up at the small graveyard in the church at the top of the hill, no one remembered the storm, or the drink – but everyone remembered him refusing to allow Agnes to sit in her normal seat. Sometimes circumstances can be very useful allies, if you knew how to use them, and Agnes did. Of course she would never have lifted a hand to harm any fisherman, no matter how drunk and stupid. In fact most of her time and talents seemed to be spent preventing them coming to harm in spite of themselves – but that particular night she was somewhere else. Many years ago Agnes had realised that despite her good intentions and her cellar door, it was impossible to be everywhere at every time. Things happened, sometimes for the good, but usually for the bad. If she could help to address the balance all well and good – if she couldn't, well Agnes had learnt to live with herself. When she slept, she slept well.

She sat in front of the fire holding her drink and listened to the rise and fall of conversation. There seemed to be some tension in the air – people weren't being as outgoing as usual. She took a glance around just to make sure there were no strangers, or worse, no revenue men. The Three Mariners, as well as being a popular harbour side inn was also a place where deals were made, cargoes bought and sold, whether duty had been paid or not. It was well known that, from time to time the senior officers at the Customs and Excise tried to send spies into the smugglers haunts. It was a dangerous occupation - some never returned, some turned out to be smugglers themselves, and some had turned out to be downright thugs – but none of them were ever successful. Agnes reflected that the Excise Men had been scare of late. In fact ever since the King and his advisors had managed to convert their political ambitions into a full scale war with England's own American Colonies there had been a shortage of Excise men along the North Eastern Coast. Agnes had heard a whisper that most of them were concentrated down south where people feared that the Colonists alongside their French allies were actually planning to invade England. Of course no one actually believed such rumours – but such rumours spread and as they spread they get larger and more fantastic and the larger and more fantastic they get the more believable they become. Agnes knew the truth. She knew the past, she knew the present and she could make a pretty good guess at what the future held. She knew an invasion was close – but she also knew it would never happen, but the locals didn't and tonight the locals were decidedly nervous.

"There's strangers about" a voice almost whispered in her ear.

Agnes didn't look around. She inclined her head towards the speaker whom, by his accent and manner of speaking belonged to Salmon Martin, a local fisherman whose nickname had nothing to do with his prowess with the nets. It was because he looked like a salmon, his mouth turned downwards in the manner of someone who has just bitten into a large piece of bait with a hook on the end, and his eyes were large and round.

"Up to no good!" continued the voice. Agnes didn't bother to ask how he knew. The locals had keen eyes. What with their dependence upon the weather and the need to avoid the excise officers they needed to.

Agnes nodded slowly. Two more figures sidled up to her and joined in the whispered conversation.

"They're not seamen either!" added one of the newcomers

Agnes looked up at the newcomers. They were locals, she could tell by the smell of oil and old fish that stained their handmade pullovers that in both cases must have had at least half a dozen previous owners. She tried to put names to the faces.

"Handy Michael, and this is our Edgar!" One of them said in answer to her raised eyebrow.

Agnes nodded as a familiar memory drifted into place. They were two of the men who worked on the dock hauling in the catch and helping the fishermen get their catch to the market. Despite the fact that the fish market was on the side of the harbour it still needed a deal of muscle and manpower to hoist the wicker baskets full of writhing, silver darlings out of the boats and drag them to the women who would wash and gut them before placing them in large barrels ready to go under the mornings hammer. Herring were fetching a good price at the moment. The war had created problems with getting goods in and out of the southern ports and had driven up the price of northern fish. It was said that the French had blockaded most of the south coast. Agnes reflected on how a war so very far away could affect life at home. These days there was an endless procession of carts and wagons leaving the port and heading inland to the larger cities, hungry for fish. No sooner had they been pickled and cured than they were sent off heading over the turnpike roads leading to York and Leeds.

"And they're not from the garrison either." Salmon Martin added, nodding towards the inns smoke stained and grimy windows and beyond, out of the inn, up the hill towards the headland where a barracks had been housed among the ruins of the much older castle.

Agnes emptied her mug and held it up. A hand took it from her and almost instantly replaced it with a full one. Agnes gave an inner smile. She had their respect, something that was always good for a few free drinks, after all there had to be some perks to being known as "wize" woman.

"How do you know – I hear there's a lot of new troopers around." She answered.

"They don't walk like army men". Edgar added.

"Nor navy." added his brother.

Agnes nodded. "I'll keep a weather eye open for them. See what I can make of it."

Job done the men around her gave a satisfactory nod and returned to their various conversations about the state of the fishing and the state of the weather and the state of everything else that touched their lives. Agnes listened politely for a while before drinking up and leaving.

As she walked back up the steps towards her house she paused and looked up between the tightly pressed buildings into the small patch of night sky. She sniffed, she could sense trouble in the air. It was as if the small town was holding its breath, waiting for something to happen. The hairs on the back of her neck began to tingle – her sixth sense was giving herself a warning – and Agnes never ignored a warning. It went with the job.

That night, back in the 21st century, she pottered around in her library pulling out books, cross-referencing entries and articles, checking and rechecking. She sat in her chair and made a movement with her hands and a computer screen appeared, she surfed the net searching, reading, cross checking until she found the information she wanted. She then flipped over to a supermarket web site and placed an order. Well a woman has to eat.

Eventually she went to bed. Yes an event was due but, as ever, her part in it remained a mystery. She could never really work out if it was a blessing or a curse that witches could not predict their own future. It was bad enough trying to predict the actions of others. She had never gone in for fortune telling – oh she could pick up hints here and there, a change in a persons' body aura, a look in their face, but that was the ability to read character, not the future. She could tell if someone was ill, and she could judge the seriousness of that illness – but that wasn't fortune telling either, today, in the 21st century it was called preventative medicine.

Hindsight is a wonderful thing, but history is history. Events must run their due course, the past could never be changed, but little bits of history, that was something else. No one had ever recorded the little bits of history, the things that happened that, in the grand scheme of things proved inconsequential, except for the people it happened to, and whilst they could never be altered, they could be jarred, a life could be saved here, a situation could be bettered there. The mere fact it happened made it happen. She knew full-well that world history could never be changed by a witch no matter how old she was, no matter how much previous knowledge she had. No a witches role was to look after the little things. Look after pennies and the pounds will look after themselves, ran the saying. In the case of historical events Agnes looked after the people that fought hard to get hold of the pennies.

Agnes enjoyed history – after all she had lived through most of it, and had been able to experience it at first hand. She also enjoyed reading about it, in the comfort of her own home. It constantly surprised her how many times the historians had got it wrong. Sometime during the previous decade Agnes even signed herself up to an Open University course. She'd never had a formal education and thought that having letters behind her name would be an interesting experience. She only lasted half a term. It was the essay about the construction of the Whitby to Pickering railway line that did for her. In order to understand the route planning process she'd walked through her cellar wall and arrived at Grosmont on the day a Mr George Stevenson and his son set out to walk the route. She'd followed on behind and struck up a conversation with the pioneering engineer. Subtly she'd picked his brain until she had the answers she wanted. Back home she recorded every last detail and spent hours carefully crafting this detail into her essay.

It came as a huge shock to her when she was told she had failed the module on the grounds of her over imagination. There were no records of the things she had written about therefore, according to the historians it was conjecture and not fact. Historians wanted facts not opinions. Agnes knew that it was the historians that had got it wrong, but, as they wrote the history, there was no arguing. The last thing Agnes could do was to announce that her paper was based on fact because she had actually been there and seen it at first hand. The historians had actually created a new truth, a truth that, over the years, became an indisputable fact, and once it became fact no one was willing to dispute it. It dawned on Agnes that all she was really expected to do was re-write and confirm the historian's opinion of how and why things had happened, she soon lost faith in the course and dropped out. Anyway she told herself, she really didn't enjoy all the writing.

The following morning the 18th century weather was still holding out. Agnes walked along the bustling harbour side where workshops and baiting sheds were squashed side by side with mast houses, coopers, inns, rigging houses, rope and sail makers. As she walked she nodded to a variety of tradesmen, fishermen, and fishwives alike. Threading her way between the drying nets, lobster pots and ropes she headed to the fish market at the end of the pier. She stopped alongside a huge trestle table where a dozen or so women were sorting and gutting last night's catch. They nodded to her as she slid an oilskin apron around her waist, rolled her sleeves up and began to expertly cut a fish down the centre of its stomach. Agnes believed in hands-on, after all to understand a community you had to be a part of it and usually being a part of it meant getting your hands dirty.

The woman's tongues were as busy as their hands and soon Agnes knew everything that was happening in and around the streets she lived in. She knew who was having trouble with the Revenue, who was having trouble paying a chandlers bill, who was stepping out with whom, who was feuding, who was expecting, and who she could expect knocking on her door in the next few weeks. She let it all pass over her – selective hearing was what she called it.

She began to pay attention when she heard one of the women declare, almost in a whisper. "He's there again!"

She looked across to where the woman had inclined her head. Sure enough there was a man standing on the corner of the street, leaning casually against a house wall puffing on a small clay pipe. He looked like a fisherman just passing the time of day until he was wanted on board again, but Agnes noticed his position was carefully chosen, from where he was stood, not only could he see what was happening along the foreshore but also look up the hill along the only street that led down from the town to the harbour. She also noticed that Salmon Martin was right, despite his clothing, the man wasn't a sailor.

"His mates been hanging around the Newcastle Packet for the past half hour" another woman's voice added.

Agnes looked down the road. Sure enough there was another man leaning against the wall of the public house. Agnes wasn't sure but by the way his coat was hanging she would be willing to bet that there was a pistol tucked away inside the left hand side. She realised he must be right handed – it was funny the little things you noticed. She looked again as a third stranger walked down the street – this figure must have already walked past the man standing on the corner. She looked to see if there was any acknowledgement between him and the man she had been watching.

There was. If you hadn't been looking for it you wouldn't have seen it – it was just the slight raising of an eyebrow, as he passed. After a brief pause the standing man began following. She looked back down the street. Sure enough the third man was also following on behind. Agnes took off her apron and slipped into an alleyway. She waited until he'd walked past then slipped out onto the foreshore and began to walk after them.

Keeping her distance she followed them as they turned to the right and walked, in single file, up Castlegate which, as it name implied, led uphill to a small church, a number of better class dwellings, and the entrance to the Castle that towered above them on the headland, currently guarded by two very bored looking soldiers. However instead of heading towards the entrance of the Castle, the men turned quickly into the surrounding undergrowth and disappeared from view.

Agnes didn't fancy following them. She figured that there was more than a possibility that she had been seen and the last thing she needed was to be dragged into the gorse bushes to have her throat cut. She turned and walked back down the hill, made a quick turn, and slipped through her own front door.

As she stood in her 21st century kitchen waiting for the kettle to boil she heard a crash and a rattle behind her. Without looking around she knew her cat had forced his way through the cat flap and, by the way he was rubbing up against her leg, wanted feeding. She opened a packet of food, carefully placed in into a saucer and placed it on the floor. The cat sniffed it with disdain and looked up at her. She went to her cupboard and found a tin of sardines. She opened them and poured them into a different saucer and was greeted by a deep satisfied purr as the cat gobbled them up.

As the cat licked the saucer clean Agnes sat back drinking her tea from a mug that graphically proclaimed its owner as - "The World's Best Granny", a gift from one of the neighbours little girls. Well actually it had been bought by the little girl's mother, who mistakenly saw in Agnes an opportunity for a built-in baby sitter. Agnes liked children, but not so much that she actually wanted to spend any time with them. Eventually she had to give the mother one of her special looks that left the mother wondering whether she should call social services to help look after an old woman that was so obviously incapable of looking after herself, let alone a neighbour's child. Needless to say the subject had never cropped up again.

Agnes directed her mind from children and mugs and moved onto the more pressing question of why three strangers would be interested in crawling about in the undergrowth beneath the Castle walls. It was possible that they were tinkers or smugglers, however their clothing suggested that they weren't men who had fallen on hard times and were living rough. Also gorse bushes weren't exactly the best place to stay and there was lot better rough sleeping to be had just about anywhere other than the steeply inclined castle banks. There had to be a reason they were there and Agnes knew she had to know it.

That night she slipped back in time, back to the Three Mariners and voiced her worries to Whitby John, Salmon Martin and Edgar. They agreed it was "A bit rum!" They promised Agnes that when they had a chance they would take a walk up to the Castle and have a look around. As she walked home she looked up at the forbidding Castle. In the gloom she thought she could just make out the light of a lantern moving around under the castle wall.

The next day she stayed at home mixing up potions and catching up on housework. The first action had actually led to the second. Agnes was a passable cook, and could mix up potions along with the best of them. Agnes's problem was her inability to cope with her microwave oven. The result wasn't exactly an explosion – it was more of an eruption that caused the microwave door to fly across the room and left a strange green gloop hanging from her ceiling that was powerful enough to strip the paintwork. The cat fled through the cat flap.

"To hell with technology!" she thought to herself as she stepped through the wall into a period where she could revert to the old fashioned, but more stable sort of technology offered by her old trusty cauldron. What with the mixing and cooling and the subsequent cleaning of the kitchen it was the following day before she slipped back in time and emerged in the 18th century.

As soon as she stepped into the street she knew something wasn't right. There was an atmosphere. She was halfway down Castlegate when she passed one of the fisherwoman walking quickly in the opposite direction. It was obvious to anyone with eyes that she had been crying. As soon as the woman saw Agnes she ran up with her hands to her face.

"Have you heard – it's awful – awful…"

Agnes waited as another deep sob shook the woman's body.

"It's Sammy Storr – they found him this morning at the bottom of the headland. His head was all caved in, they say he must have fallen from the cliff – said he must have been trying to collect gulls eggs."

She paused to take breath. Agnes patted her on the shoulder.

"Where is the body?" asked the ever practical Agnes

"The Constable came and arranged for it to go to the hospital."

Agnes nodded. "If you need anything you know where I am." She offered.

The woman nodded her head. "I'm off around to the Storrs, see if there's owt I can do… poor thing it were only last year she lost her eldest in that storm, now to lose her youngest!"

Agnes nodded. "Is her husband still with the Army?" she asked

The woman sniffed and wiped her nose on her sleeve. "Aye, last I heard he was in the Americas, fighting for General Howe. Who knows, he could be dead. Killed as we're stood speaking here!"

"Aye, it's looking on the bright side that keeps us going!" commented Agnes.

The woman looked up defensively. "Well you can never tell. Face it, she's been unlucky with her two sons."

"Yes…. Two sons in as many years. I have a feeling that Mrs Storr will be finding the world a hard place right now. Tell her I'll pop around in a while." Before the woman could say anything else Agnes turned and headed off down to the harbour.

Despite the fact that news always travels fast inside a small community, and bad news even quicker, it took her the best part of an hour to put the complete story together. From what she could gather it seemed that a fishing boat had been laying its nets just under the headland at first light when the crew had noticed something slumped on the nearby rocks, directly under the cliff. They sailed as near to the rocks as was possible where they could make out that the shape was the body of a man but, as the tide was on the turn, they couldn't reach it from the boat. They quickly finished laying their nets and returned to the harbour to raise the alarm. The local constable immediately raised the few men he could find and together they walked under the headland on the small strip of land and, by jumping from rock to rock, they found the body. It was quickly identified as that of Samuel Storr by various members of the rescue party.

She found one of them in the Three Mariners. Before he took to life behind the bar of the Mariners Whitby John had been a fisherman – but the lure of the sea never really appealed. As she walked up to him cleaning the tankards she cast a glance at the cloth he was using and gave an inward shudder, it was covered in a sort of greasy slime and looked as if it had cleaned a thousand tankards too many.

"Ever thought of investing in a new cloth?" She thought aloud.
Whitby John looked and gave her a nod of recognition. He ignored her comment and reached for another tankard to smear. "I had a feeling you'd be here."

Never one to beat about the bush Agnes went to the heart of her enquiries. "Is it true what I heard?"

He gave a shrug. "Depends on what you heard. If you heard I helped to pull a body off the rocks? Yes. If you heard that he fell off the cliff – no."

Agnes raised an eyebrow. The man finished wiping the tankard and placed it on a shelf behind the bar. He wiped his hands with the cloth and placed it on the counter before leaning forward. "They say he was collecting eggs. But Sammy Storr didn't go in for egg collecting – he didn't like heights."

Agnes digested the news. "So what do you think he was he doing up on the cliff?"

The barmen leant even further over and lowered his voice. "Well, we all know you were interested in them three strangers." She raised another eyebrow.

He gave another shrug. "It's common knowledge that you asked 'em all to keep an eye on 'em. As soon as you left the pub was full of talk. You know the sort of thing, who are they, why are they here, why's Agnes interested in them…."

Agnes sighed. In fairness to the fishermen she had never actually said it was a secret – but, as always, a little knowledge can a be a dangerous thing – especially if that knowledge only reveals a partial picture, and especially when it gets magnified by alcohol.

John continued "Eventually we all decided to keep a weather eye open, including Sammy. Anyway day a'for yesterday Pete came down from the Castle – he'd been up at the garrison on some business or other and decided to walk down the embankments, you know just to have a look around."

He paused to allow Agnes to digest this news. When she didn't say anything he continued. "Seems he found the remains of a small camp fire. Reckoned that folks must have been living up there. Anyway after Sammy's body had been found Pete took a couple of the lads back up. Only this time there was no sign of the camp. Not a trace, no ashes, not even a burnt bit of wood. They'd covered their tracks."

"What was Sammy doing up there in the first place?"

The barman straightened up and rubbed the base of his back. "Rabbits – Sammy used to go up there most weeks, take a bit of netting with him and catch rabbits – a pair of fat coneys fetches a good price."

Agnes nodded. The large rabbit population up on the embankments was well known, but she had never realised that the locals had their own method of population control. "Where did he sell them?"

He grinned. "Oh here and there, here for a start, and he had his regular customers. Just because the folk round here catch fish don't mean we have to live off the stuff all the time. Bit of stewed rabbit makes a nice change."

Agnes suddenly remembered a rather nice rabbit pie she'd been given a few months earlier as a payment for some tincture she'd made up. She also remembered that at the time, she'd never given a thought as to where the rabbits had actually come from.

"Did he sell any to the garrison?" She asked.

John laughed. "You're joking – even poor old Sammy wouldn't have had the nerve to sell the army their own rabbits back."

Agnes was surprised. "Their rabbits?"

"Oh aye, the powers that be up there reckon anything on the Castle banks is the property of the army."

"Do they keep an eye out for poachers then?"

John shook his head. "Now Missus – let's make this clear a'for anyone says owt a'ginst a dead man. Sammy wasn't a poacher – them rabbits were here afore the army, aye and they'll be here after they've gone – they're not the army's rabbits, they're ours. But no, they don't guard the warren. In fact if truth be known, they don't guard much up there. Oh don't get me wrong – they guard the entrance obviously, and the roadway – but their job is to keep them guns aimed out to sea. That's where everyone knows the enemy is. All their eyes are trained to look seawards. Anyway they've got great stone walls around them and they're perched on top of that damn great headland – no enemy is stupid enough to think they can march an army up that hill. Only way in is from the road and like I said that's guarded. It's been safe a lot of years has that castle – and it'll be safe for a lot more!"

Agnes nodded. "So no one at the Castle would spot someone camping right below their own walls?"

John paused to think for a few seconds before answering. "Not if them that was doing the camping didn't want 'em to know."

Agnes still had to be sure, she tested the theory. "Suppose Sammy was after his rabbits after all and simply slipped and fell off the headland?"

John shook his head "Like I said, he didn't go round the headland – too nervous of the height for one thing…"

"And another…?" added Agnes when John's pause began to stretch out too long, even for dramatic effect.

"Rabbits don't dig their warrens out on the headland – too much rock, not enough cover – he just wouldn't be on that part of the cliff."

Accidentally Agnes spoke her next thought out aloud. She hadn't meant to. "So how did he fall?"

John thought he'd been invited to offer his opinion. He hadn't, but that was the problem with speaking aloud, people thought you were talking to them. Agnes listened anyway.

"It's obvious. He must have stumbled across them strangers and found summat they didn't like him finding, so they silenced him."

Despite it being an obvious answer, it still posed a lot of questions. "Without any proof it's just a theory."

Theory or not John wasn't going to let his opinion be dismissed so lightly. "That's as maybe, but it would explain the nasty bump he had on the back of his head."

Agnes let out another little sigh. Sometimes stating the obvious was the obvious thing to do. "John, the poor lad, was found under the cliff. That's at least a hundred feet. I would expect his body to be broken and, I dare say, covered in nasty bumps!"

Offended by the suggestion that he could mistake a bump on the head for a injury caused by a bad fall John turned defensive. "Look missus, I'm just saying what I saw – I reckon that bump on his head wasn't caused by no fall. I've seen a fair bit of death in my time and I reckon he was hit a'fore he fell."

Agnes sat back and tried to take it all in. The last thing she wanted to do was question John, for a fisherman turned bar man he was very well informed. There again she reminded herself, anyone working in the Three Mariners for a couple of weeks would know just about everything there was to know about the fishing community. Or at least what the fishing community thought was good enough for them to know.

"I'll ask around." she replied

John raised an eyebrow.

Agnes sighed. "I said, I'll ask around!"

John nodded and returned to his attempts at cleaning the tankards.

She left the Mariners and made her way back up the hill. Taking a slight diversion she stopped by Mrs Storrs. The bereft mother was surrounded by concerned neighbours and various family offering comfort and sympathy. Agnes knew she'd be alright, for now. It was when they all returned to their own lives that the realisation would sink in and that was when Agnes would call. She left the house as quietly as she entered but on the way out she saw a pile of washing and quickly slipped an item of clothing under her coat. She made her way down the narrow street and headed towards her own front door.

Back home she slipped forward in time and used her electric kettle to make a cup of tea and switched onto BBC Radio Three to provide some background music. She had decided a long time ago that the 21st century was a very convenient place to live and she enjoyed the little luxuries its technology offered. She knew she could flick her fingers and a kettle would boil, or the tea would be made, but she didn't like using magic for everyday. Anyway her own tea wasn't a patch on that made by someone called Tetley, and she'd always liked music. She just had to remind herself not to whistle the greatest hits of Tom Jones when she was back in the 18th century, or any other century for that matter. That way history could be changed and that would cause no end of problems, and she didn't like problems.

As she sipped her tea her mind turned over question after question. Who were the strangers? Were there only three of them? Why were they living rough up at the castle? The answer to that question seemed one of the more obvious ones, they didn't want people to know they were there. But what were they up to and what was so important that they were willing to kill to keep their secret safe? Whoever they were they must be dangerous. She knew needed to do something.

She pulled out the piece of clothing she had "borrowed" from the Storrs house. It turned out to be a thick woollen fisherman's sock. She smiled at her good fortune for finding it in the clean pile of washing. Placing the sock on her lap, she put her hands over it, simply closed her eyes, and let her mind go.

She never could find the right words to describe what exactly it was that she did. However as she never spoke to anyone about it, finding the right words really wasn't a problem. Some might call it scrying but in her own mind she called it seeping. She just allowed her mind to seep out and merge with…well whatever it was it merged with. It seeped out of the chair, out of her room and out of the house heading out over the castle banks. If it was visible Agnes suspected it would look like a thin grey mist.

It wasn't long before she picked up some traces, shadow memories, lurking among the gorse and undergrowth. She found hidden traces of the stranger's camp and traces of the late Sammy Storr. She found some nets hidden under a gorse bush. Then she found a second set apparently discarded, laying out in the open. Something told her a poacher wouldn't leave his nets where anyone could find them. She drifted further up towards the castle wall and allowed her mind to travel across its base, where the medieval stonework was buried deep in the earth.

She almost missed it at first. It had been well hidden. There, behind the tangle of a huge gorse bush, was a large hole that seemed to be tunnelled downwards, under the wall itself. At first glance it could easily pass as a badgers den. It was certainly too big for rabbits, but that fact could be easily missed by someone who was laying nets under the cover of darkness. She winced slightly as she passed over the spot where Sammy had been hit over the head. She found the bent grass and track where his unconscious body had been dragged round to the headland, and she found the spot that they had thrown him from. For someone wishing to dispose of a body it had been a good choice, it was almost a sheer drop to the rocks and the sea below. But the attackers had made one mistake. Sammy couldn't have fallen from that point, no one in their right mind would have attempted to trap rabbits on such a cliff face.

She opened her eyes and waited a couple of minutes as she felt the seeping return to her. She took another sip of tea and was surprised to discover it had gone cold. She walked back into the kitchen and turned the kettle on. As she threw more of Mr Tetley's tea bags into the pot and waited for the kettle to boil she summarised her discoveries.

Strangers had dug a hole under the castle wall. They had been disturbed by Sammy and they had killed him to prevent their secret from being discovered. Experience told her that any further explorations and investigations into three killers could possibly get dangerous. So far in her scrying she had only come across the traces of three men, but were they the same three men she had seen a couple of days previously. If so at least one of them was armed. She tried to remember their faces and their clothing. Nothing stood out. She wondered who they were working for, and how many others were in their pay? She knew that if the strangers were so desperate as to kill a fisherman turned poacher they wouldn't stop at hurting a frail old woman and although danger didn't worry her, she knew her limitations, magical and physical. For years it was a common belief that a witch could summon up a magical fireball or change an attacker into a frog, but those spells take time and effort. Agnes knew only too well that a man armed with a pistol or knife was a lot faster than a witch armed with just a spell. No this situation called for a more drastic approach than one that could be offered by just a little old lady. It called for the assistance of the little old ladies cat.

Agnes emptied her cup and peered out of the kitchen window. Marmaduke, her cat was in his usual position, asleep in a puddle of sunshine on top of the green wheelie bin. Silently Agnes slipped on a pair of old leather gauntlets and tip-toed into the yard. She picked the cat up very gently and marched towards the cellar. As she opened the door Marmaduke open his one good eye, quickly assessed the situation, decided he didn't like it and dug his claws into Agnes' forearm. They made no impression on the aged leather and suddenly he found himself being spun around and thrown directly at the cellar wall. Agnes counted to ten before following him through.

As she stepped back into the 18th century there was no sign of the angry cat. Instead there stood a very angry man. He was well built, ginger haired with a fine long moustache and pointed beard. One ear was half missing and a black eye patch covered his blind eye. He wore long leather knee boots and a leather jerkin that covered a loose fitting shirt through which you could just make out a scarred but tanned chest. To all intent he looked like a rake, a letch, a leery and disreputable pirate, someone whom after you've shaken his hand you'd instinctively count your fingers, a man you would definitely go a long way to avoid upsetting, especially after you noticed his smile. It wasn't a grin, it was more like a couple of very thin lips pulled tight across a set of very fine, and very pointed teeth. There was something about his hands as well. His fingers were short and stubby and his fingernails were filed into small sharp points.

He stood in front of Agnes stretching his arms and moving his legs like a person who had fallen asleep in a very hard chair and was trying to regain the feeling in their limbs. Every so often he'd turn around very quickly. When he spoke he still had traces of a cat's voice, or how one would imagine a cat would speak if it could.

"I really do wish you would give me some warning." He complained.

"If I gave you warning you wouldn't go through the wall!" replied Agnes

"That's what I mean." replied Marmaduke quickly turning around once again.

"It's not there you know." Said Agnes, trying not to smile.

"I know – it's just…disconcerting. One minute you've a nice tail stretching out behind you, the next minute you're on your hind legs and your tails missing. It takes some getting used to. It throws your balance right out."

"I think a tail would spoil the overall effect." replied Agnes

"I like my tail. It's a good tail." Marmaduke said still looking behind him.

"For a cat…." Said Agnes

"Well yes…"

Agnes quickly changed the subject. "I suppose you're hungry!"

"I always am." He replied as he scratched behind his ear with his left hand.

She led the way back to the kitchen and instinctively reached towards the cupboard where the cat food was stored. Marmaduke gave a cough that could be said to be just this side of politeness. Agnes realised her mistake.

"Sardines on toast?" She asked quickly.

"Is the toast really necessary?" Marmaduke looked around.

"Yes, and so is a knife and fork." She replied firmly. Marmaduke knew better than to disagree.

As she watched him devour the meal she explained the events of the last few days. She went over the arrival of the strangers, the death of Sammy Storr, her suspicions and her ideas. Marmaduke finished eating and sat back. His tongue flicked over his moustache once or twice and he began to scratch behind his ear with his hand. Agnes raised an eyebrow. Marmaduke gave a shrug –

"It does take time to adjust you know." He replied

"Maybe, but I wouldn't try it in public. They don't go in for licking their own faces around here."

Marmaduke gave a smile. "You'd be surprised."

Agnes tried to ignore the comment and failed. Inwardly she gave a little shudder as she imagined what he got up to as a cat. Unfortunately she had a very vivid imagination.

"So, you want me to find these three strangers?" He asked after some minutes of silence, hoping he could distract Agnes from whatever it was that she was thinking about. The look of horror that had appeared on her face was so alarming he'd turned and looked behind him twice.

Agnes managed to shake various images from her head. "I didn't think it was possible for even a cat to bend like that… Sorry what were you saying? Find the strangers? Yes, yes of course we must find the strangers, I want to know what they're doing and why they're digging holes under our castle."

"A hole!" Stated Marmaduke.

"What?" Agnes leant forward in hr chair as if she hadn't heard him properly

Marmaduke repeated himself. "A hole. As far as you know they've only dug one hole. You said holes, plural."

"Oh... I never thought about them digging other holes. I wonder…"

"You want I should go and have a look around?" Offered Marmaduke.
"I think that would be for the better. I should have carried on looking, but it never…"

Her words trailed off. She should have looked. Was she getting old and forgetful? Or was it that once she'd found the shadow traces of Sammy Storr she'd thought that was that. I've made a mistake she thought to herself. That's careless, that's not like me. Her line of thought was interrupted.

Marmaduke was looking out of the small kitchen window. "I think I'd prefer to wait till it gets dark." He turned to face Agnes. "In the meanwhile stop worrying about not thinking about everything at the same time. Any chance of some more sardines – without toast this time?"

When darkness fell over the town Marmaduke slipped out of the back door and silently moved his way through the gorse and bracken up the Castle banks. He found the hole easily. He examined the old stonework around the hole and then looked up to where the edge of the wall merged with the night sky. It was climbable but you'd need ladders, or a grappling iron and rope at the very least. But there again he reasoned, if you were planning on climbing over a wall, you wouldn't be digging a hole under it.

He continued moving careful along the base of the wall stopping every so often and examining the ground and the stonework. By the time he had followed the curve of the wall all the way round until he was on the castle headland he'd found another two holes. Both of them were the same size as the original. He looked down the cliff, to where the sea was lapping against the rocks far below. It was a good job he had a cats head for heights. A kittiwake screamed abuse at him as he found a place to rest. The rocks round here were not that stable and he steadied himself as he sat down. Even in his human form he had a feeling he'd be able to land on his feet, but he wasn't that eager to test the theory, especially from a hundred feet up. Without thinking he found he had picked up a stone. He just managed to stop himself from throwing it at a nearby seagull sat on its nest. Instinct is hard to overcome and in his cat form Marmaduke had experienced a number of set to's with the local seagulls. In fact he'd lost the tip of one of his ears to one of the vicious birds. He reminded himself he was human, put the stone down carefully and looked out to sea.

Being sat on the end of the headland he could see into both of the bays that almost met behind him, threatening to cut off the castle from the mainland. To the north the bay swept away gently on a large flat and sandy beach before ending in a series of cliffs and headlands that stretched all the way up the coast to Whitby.

In the opposite direction he could look down into the South Bay, home of the harbour, the old town and its myriad of fishing related industries house in various sheds and huts, right along the foreshore, and up to the road that led to the The Spaw, a fashionable spot where visitors from all over Britain came to taste the waters, and enjoy the newly created recreation of sea bathing. Marmaduke gave a little shiver. He had a cat's natural instinct for the dislike of water, and the thought of bathing in the sea was alien to him. Beyond the Spaw the bay stretched south. In the darkness he could just make out the shape of a second bay and the coast as it curved all the way towards Filey and beyond.

Looking out to sea, over the calm waters he could see the lights on the boats bobbing up and down as the fishermen threw or gathered in their nets and lines. That night the South Bay seemed to be full of small boats. He turned his head, there were very few fishing in the North Bay. Suddenly a small flashing light caught his eye. It appeared as if it was coming from a boat that was more northerly. Further away than the end of the North Bay. Marmaduke watched as the small pin-prick of light flashed on and off, on and off. He scratched behind his ear. It looked as if it was signalling. Of course he knew full well that up and down the coast all manner of illegal activity was going on. It was probably a small ketch running a cargo that wouldn't be bothering the customs men. He estimated that it must be off the coast somewhere near to a village called Cloughton that lay about four miles from the castle. A handy place to drop off an illegal cargo. Up there the sea was guarded by steep cliffs cut into by small inlets that provided safe havens, if you knew how to avoid the rocks and tides. Tobacco, spices, silks, gin, anything could be dropped off secretly in any number of small inlets and, once ashore, easily transported inland across secret moorland tracks until it found its way into the more normal distribution networks to be transported to waiting merchants in the larger cities of Leeds and York.

He stood up, stretched and began to carefully circle back under the castle wall and made his way back home. When he let himself into the house he found Agnes apparently asleep in her easy chair. He knew better than to wake her and made his way into the kitchen to look for more sardines. As he searched through the cupboard he pondered on how life as a cat would be so very different if only evolution had given them thumbs. They would be able to open their own tins for a start.

"If you're making a pot of tea…I've got some scones." said a voice behind him. Marmaduke turned and sniffed suspiciously at the scones. Agnes didn't do baking.

"Mrs Pickard dropped them by in exchange for a potion to help ride her husband of that nasty cough he's had all winter. Three hundred years old and fresh this morning."

She smiled and spread a large dollop of jam over one of them in the same way a bricklayer spread mortar over a brick.

Marmaduke declined the added jam option. He knew from experience that jam could play havoc with a set of well-groomed whiskers. Instead, as he licked the butter off, he began to tell what he'd found. He didn't get very far.

"I know. I followed you." replied Agnes.

Marmaduke raised an eyebrow.

Agnes shook her head. "Not physically – I… well let's just say I was with you in spirit."

Marmaduke knew better than to ask Agnes about her talents. She did what she did, when she needed to do it. He didn't understand it and he didn't want to. He preferred his life to be simple, after all he was a cat. As long as was fed and warm and kept jam free he was happy.

"That boat was interesting." She added.
Marmaduke finished his tea and began to lick the inside of the cup. "Just smugglers."

Agnes tried to ignore Marmaduke's table manners. "I thought that at first, then I took a closer look. You wouldn't have seen it from your position on the cliff but someone was signalling from the shore, then they landed, somewhere north of Cloughton."

"Like I said, smugglers." Marmaduke's words echoed from inside the cup.

"But local smugglers don't usually deal with guns. It's out of their league." replied Agnes

He stopped licking the cup and looked up. "Guns?" he repeated.

Agnes carefully took the cup out of Marmaduke's hand and walked towards the sink with it. "The cargo they were running was packed in two crates – inside the crates were rifles." She said as she rinsed the cup out under the tap.

Marmaduke shrugged. "Well it makes a change from gin and tea."

Agnes made a disapproving sound by clicking her teeth as she held the cup up to the light making sure it was clean. "No, you're not understanding what I'm saying. Why rifles – who would want to buy rifles around here?"

Marmaduke finished off his the scone in one gulp. "You know this lot round here. If the price is right they'd buy anything."

"Stop thinking like a cat. There's no one around here that could afford to buy that amount of guns. Two crates, each containing a dozen rifles? There's not twenty four people round here with that sort of money."

Marmaduke thought for a moment. "What about the garrison?"

Agnes gave a little snort "They're issued with guns, they get them free, there wouldn't be anyone left in the army if they had to buy their own guns."

Marmaduke began to inspect his finger nails. "Speaking of the garrison. I noticed something up at the Castle. Those holes they dug. Did you realise that each of them are dug directly under the gun emplacements."

Agnes smiled "Mmm I had wondered about that."

Marmaduke wasn't convinced. "Really?"

Agnes ignored the hint of sarcasm "Yes really. After you discovered where they were I got to thinking and thought I'd better take a look so I allowed myself to drift over the walls."

"You drifted inside the Garrison?"

Agnes. "I can you know. I had a look at the cannon. You're right. The holes are directly under them. I wouldn't mind betting that there's some gunpowder laying around somewhere."

Marmaduke repeated the word. "Gunpowder?"

"You're still thinking like a cat." Agnes said. "Gunpowder. You know, stuff that is used to blow things up with. I think someone wants to fill those holes with it and put a match to it."

Marmaduke patted behind his ears again. "It would take a lot of gunpowder to blow those walls up. More than you could get into those holes."

Agnes wasn't listening, she sat back in her chair with pursed lips. "Of course, as well as rifles, the smugglers must have brought some gunpowder with them. Come to think about it, there were some small casks on the boat. At the time I thought it was brandy."

Marmaduke continued with scratching his ears and the back of his head. "Like I said, they would have to be big barrels to hold enough gunpowder to knock down those walls."

Agnes leant forward and resisted the urge to knock Marmaduke's hands from his head. "Not enough to blow the walls down. But enough to cause considerable damage to below where the cannons are placed. Those things need to be pointing in a straight line. If they were disturbed, let's say by a big explosion, they just might point downwards, and that wouldn't be any good, unless they wanted to fire on the town."

"You think someone's planning on attacking the Castle?"

"It looks like that."

"But they'd never get inside…"

Agnes stood up and began to pace up and down the kitchen. Sometimes she could think better when walking around. "Perhaps they don't want to capture the castle – perhaps they just want to disable the guns."

Marmaduke watched her pace in the faint hope that her movement would somehow equate to food preparation. "Why, what good would that do?"

"A lot of good if there's an enemy ship out there ready to attack."

"Attack the town? Why would a ship even attempt to….." he paused as he realised who he was talking to. "Just a minute, you know something don't you?"

Agnes stopped and brushed some invisible crumbs from the front of her dress. "Of course I know something. Time travel does give one the advantage of knowing what's going to happen next. That and a bit of research on the computer."

Marmaduke began scratching behind his ears again, this time with both hands. The ins and outs of time travel confused him. As far as he was concerned it was something that happened but it was something he never questioned. The answers gave him headaches. Computers had the same effect.

Agnes watched as he scratched his ears. "Do you have to keep doing that?"

Marmaduke put his hands down again. "It's a cat thing. It helps me think".

"And what were you thinking?"

A frown crossed Marmaduke's forehead as he struggled to put the words and thoughts together. Concepts of time were a bit difficult for cats to cope with. "I was thinking that if something's already happened, then there's nothing you can do to stop it, because it's already happened."

Agnes smiled. "Ah, but supposing it happened the way it did because we did something that allowed it to happen."

Marmaduke frowned again and spoke slowly. "But, if you did something to make something happen, then you'd already know about it, because you'd already done it and you'd remember it!"

Now it was Agnes' turn to frown. "I'm not sure it works like that."

"OK then, how does it work?"

Agnes sighed, this was going to take some explaining, especially to someone who spent most of his time as a cat. "Look at it this way. In the 1770's, that is now, it's happening for me for the first time."

"Us!" Marmaduke interrupted.

The interruption broke Agnes's train of thought. "Sorry?"

"Us." repeated Marmaduke. "It's happening to us for the first time."

Agnes acknowledged he had a point. "Sorry, it's happening to us for the first time. Oh yes, I can look up what happened, I can read the history books, I can check on-line, but that only provides the broad brushstrokes. There's a lot of history that's never written down, and if it's not written down people forget, and it stops being history. Those unknown bits are the bits that I… sorry we, can affect."

Marmaduke narrowed his eyes and began to scratch furiously behind his ears again. "Are you saying that history happened the way it did because you did whatever it is you're planning to do?"

Agnes sighed. "Ah now that's the problem. I'm not too sure what I should be doing."

Marmaduke turned and began to lick his shoulder. Agnes watched as his tongue darted across the lapel of his jacket. "I do know you shouldn't be doing that though!"

"It's a cat thing. The more you try to explain the more I'm glad I'm just a cat, and the more I think like a cat the more I act like one." He said as he "pawed" himself faster and faster.

"Well don't go acting like that in public. People tend to get a bit funny with other people licking themselves. Especially there!" she added hastily.

They sat in silence. Marmaduke eventually gave up his feline grooming and curled up on the table with his head resting on his arms and began to drift off to sleep. The last words he heard were Agnes saying softly, "Anyway I have a plan."

Chapter Two

The following morning saw Agnes making her way along the foreshore nodding to acquaintances here and there. Marmaduke had set off much earlier. A carrier service left town at seven o'clock, by nine he would be passing through the village of Cloughton. As the cart passed through the outskirts of the town Marmaduke sat on the back allowing his legs to dangle over the edge and lay on his back watching the sky pass overhead.

The carrier knew Agnes and owed her a couple of favours for some potions she had mixed up for him. She had intended them to cure a severe case of heartburn, that she had diagnosed but, despite Agnes saying otherwise, the carrier was convinced that it was his heart that had been affected. Then he had taken the medicine and shortly afterwards met a widow woman. The two had struck up a liking for each other that led to them walking out and eventually to a happy marriage. Ever since then the carrier went around telling anyone who was interested that Agnes had not only cured his aching heart but that she had concocted a love potion that had attracted his new wife and was the cause of his eternal happiness. Agnes knew better, she knew dyspepsia when she saw it, but a good word never hurt anyone and it was useful to know that she could always call on the services of a carrier when she needed one.

Down by the harbour Agnes walked towards a large stone building with a doorway at the side that opened up to reveal a ships chandlers. The owner was another local man in her debt and she was about to call it in. Andrew Marks knew everything about ships. He knew how to fit them out, how to sail them and what made them work. Most of what made them work was inside his building, stored in drawers, stacked high on the shelves, or hanging from the ceiling. As she entered the shop great loops of ropes and nets swung gently above her head. On the walls a vast variety of lanterns, grappling irons, and various other tools were displayed. But Agnes wasn't shopping for a fishing net. She knew that Andrew not only knew everything there was to know about how ships work, but he also knew what use they were put to. He knew every ship that came in and out of the harbour, and their cargoes, legal or illegal.

He stopped what he was doing the moment he saw her come into the shop. As she walked across the shop floor he turned to his assistant and asked him to take charge. Then he gently took Agnes's arm and led her to a small office at the rear of the shop. A window looking out over the harbour let in a patch of daylight that illuminated a large desk on which papers and documents were set out in various piles. A large leather bound ledger lay at their centre. Gas lights flickered on the walls and a fire glowed in a small hearth. The room smelt of a mixture of tobacco smoke and grease. Andrew pulled a small upholstered chair away from the wall and offered it to Agnes. She sat gratefully as he made himself comfortable behind the desk. After passing a couple of pleasantries and a making brief enquiry into her health he took a deep breath and asked if he could help her. She smiled.

"I'm interested in a boat that was seen off the coast up Cloughton way last night." She said.

Andrew thought for a moment or two before shaking his head. "Not anyone I know of."

Agnes tutted. "Come on Andrew, you know every boat that comes in and out of yon harbour. Who was out last night?"

Andrew shrugged and tried to avoid looking her in the eye. "Just the usual boats doing the usual fishing."

Agnes stared at him, hard. "Andrew, you really don't want me to remind you of who I am, do you?" She closed her eyes just for a moment and concentrated her thoughts in the direction of the shop. Then she opened her eyes and looked Andrew straight in the face. "For instance I'm sure you wouldn't like it to be known that there's three barrels of Brandy and two shots of silk in your cellar that shouldn't be there."

The colour began to drain from Andrews face "Agnes, please believe me, there wasn't a run last night. At least not one that I know about."

Agnes smiled. "That's not to mention two chests of tea and barrel of Dutch Gin!"

Andrew face had now turned a delicate shade of white. "How the…."

Agnes wasn't smiling anymore. "You know how. This is important. Please, think again."

Andrew thought again. "One of the lads did do a rundown Bridlington way."

Agnes shook her head. "Wrong direction. I'm talking north of here."

Andrew shook his head. "No, no one I know of did a run north last night, and that's Gods honest truth." He added, just in case she doubted him.

"Could anybody be doing something you didn't know about?" Agnes asked.

"It's always possible, maybe someone from further up the coast, up Whitby way or beyond, but all our lads are accounted for last night. Anyway it's a bit dangerous just now, there's a couple of Navy ships out there. One of them's newly launched, sailed up here straight from Rotherhithe."

"Do you know their names?" she enquired.
Now the subject had changed to that of the Royal Navy Andrew seemed a lot more comfortable. He flicked through the papers, pulled one towards him and read from it. "H.M.S. Serapis, a warship captained by one Richard Pearson, the others a smaller ship, "The Countess of Scarborough". No idea who her captain is. They were seen off the Humber a few days ago."

Agnes quickly put two and two together. "No doubt reported by your Bridlington runner."

Andrew pushed the paper away from him and looked up a sheepish look crossed his face. "Yes, well he did say something about it being wise to keep clear of Bridlington bay for a few days!"

"I'll bet – are they looking for smugglers?"

Andrew shook his head. "No, from what I can gather they are meant to be on convoy duty."

Agnes's ears picked up at this bit of news. "Convoy duty?"

Andrew shuffled the papers on the desk. "It's no secret. There's a merchant fleet coming in from the Baltic. A big one, about fifty ships so I heard. They're meant to have left Norway a week ago now."

Agnes made a mental calculation. "When are they due?"

"They're expected in two, maybe three days time, depending on the weather of course. They're not all bound for Scarborough though. Most of 'em are bound down south. There's only a couple of 'em due in here, carrying timber."

It was the information Agnes needed. She had suspected as much but Andrew had confirmed it. She stood up and stretched her back. "By heck Andrew, I'd get rid of that chair if it was mine. It might look good but it's not very comfortable, either that or I'm not getting any younger." She said

"Is that all?" asked Andrew, looking down at the chair. It seemed comfortable enough to him, but there again, he wasn't as wide as Agnes, but he wasn't going to risk mentioning that.

"Yes, and thank you very much. You've been most helpful." Agnes said as Andrew opened the door to let her back into the shop again. As they walked through the shop towards the street door he lent over the counter and produced a small, well-wrapped package. It was bottle shaped. Agnes raised an eyebrow.

"Dutch gin". Andrew said. Agnes smiled and popped the package into her basket.

Chapter Three

Of course the carrier had to be carrying fish.
Marmaduke could smell it. He could almost feel it
between his teeth. The effect on him was to create a
sort of fixed grin that showed his pointed teeth. It
wasn't a look that was conducive to good company.
The carrier and his horses had been uneasy the entire
journey and what little conversation he tried to initiate
tended to be about safe things like the weather and the
state of the roads. As soon as the first small cottage of
Cloughton came into view he stopped his cart. As
Marmaduke alighted the carter flicked his whip to get
the horses moving again and as he continued his
journey, gave out a huge sigh of relief

Marmaduke stood at the side of the road, watching
until the carrier disappeared down what appeared to be
the main and only street Cloughton had to offer. Once
he was out of sight Marmaduke turned away from the
village and set off down a small lane that led through
cultivated fields towards the sea and the cliff tops.
After half a mile or so it joined another track that ran
north to south along the cliff tops. Marmaduke turned
north and carried on walking through open countryside
following the small path along the cliff top before it

descended into a wood. In the distance he could make out more fields. A horse and cart stood patiently waiting as a group of workers loaded sheaves of corn. He kept low making sure he couldn't be seen. Ahead of him he could just make out the curve of the cliff top that dropped down towards a small bay nestling at the far side of the wood. Marmaduke stopped and looked behind him. In the distance he could make out the headland and the castle. He squinted as he judged the angles between the two points. This could easily be the place where last night's boat had landed.

The path that descended through the woods wasn't popular, in fact he was doubtful if it had been used in years. In places it almost lost itself among fallen trees and overgrown vegetation. Around him the trees were twisted and bent out of shape by the winds coming from the sea. Eventually it led him to a clearing on the edge of the cliff where he could look down into a small bay. Below him he could see a small waterfall that spilt over an outcrop of rock and fell ten or so feet onto a stony beach. He could also see a small boat, dragged up the beach beyond the waterline. Its mast was down and lay along the centre of the boat. A rope coiled from its bow and looped around a large rock, making the boat secure against any rising tide. He decided to sit and wait and see what, if anything would happen. The tide was on the turn and soon the sea would reach the boat. If anyone was coming back for it they would come back at high tide, when it could be launched. At least he thought, that's the theory.

He had been sitting in the bracken for an hour and despite the sea reaching further up the beach until it lapped at the bottom of the boat, the only thing he'd seen was a small bird that hopped from branch to branch just above his head. He found it was a strain not to spring up and catch it. In some far recess of his mind he could feel the thrill of the catch and a distant memory of the taste of fresh blood and feathers.

As he fought the thought out of his mind Marmaduke was suddenly aware that the birds in the wood had stopped singing. The small bird flew away chattering loudly. He dropped to his stomach and lay flattened among the bracken. He was carefully parting the fronds making sure he could still see the beach below him when he heard the movement of something further up in the wood. He listened carefully, cocking his head to one side. It was the sound of someone running. He listened to the snapping of twigs and branches. It sounded like there was more than one person running. Suddenly below him, three running figures burst out of the woods and appeared at the top of the waterfall. With hardly a look behind them each one leapt from the top of the waterfall, landed in the splash pool below and stumbled across the stony beach heading for the boat. They had almost reached it when a movement on top of the waterfall caught his eye.

Marmaduke turned his head slightly to see a solitary male figure standing at the edge of the fall. He stared. The man was dressed in a rough trews and a tunic, his face was tanned and weather beaten, two white stripes were smeared under both of his eyes, his hair was long and braided with two black feathers hanging down around its left ear. Marmaduke was fascinated, he hadn't seen the like before.

As he held his breath he watched the man standing almost motionless on the top of the waterfall. Carefully and without hurry, the man slid a bow from his shoulder. Almost in one movement he strung an arrow, aimed and fired. He repeated the action twice more. Marmaduke looked back at the beach. One of the running men had stopped and was now kneeling on the rocks looking down, puzzled at presence of an arrow sticking out of his chest. Another was lying in a crumpled heap, an arrow had ripped through his throat leaving a gaping, open wound pumping out a fountain of blood staining the rocks and pebbles around him. The third had made it to the boat but no further. He was hanging limply, his arms still gripping the side of the boat. Another arrow was sticking out of the centre of his back.

Without moving his head Marmaduke looked back at the waterfall. The archer stood on the top of the waterfall. He looked down at the figures on the beach long enough to make sure that, if they were not actually dead, none of his three victims would be leaving the beach. Finally he unstrung his bow, then turned and walked silently back into the wood and disappeared from sight.

Marmaduke waited a good ten minutes before beginning to move. Then he stood up and slowly stretched his limbs, bringing life and movement back. He flexed his muscles and just for a moment ripples ran down his body, like a cat does when it first wakes up.

He looked back towards the beach. He didn't need any medical knowledge to know that the three men were dead and there was nothing he could do for them. He turned away and very carefully he made his way down into the wood. He reached the top of the waterfall and turned inland, roughly following the direction the archer had taken. Every few paces he stopped and sniffed the air. It didn't take long before Marmaduke picked up his trail. It led inland along a steep track climbing up through the wood following the path of the stream as it rattled seawards in a gully below.

Marmaduke moved slowly and more carefully now. He could sense danger. He felt the whiskers of his moustache twitch. His hands itched and he knew that if he still had it, his tail would be swishing from side to side. Up ahead he could see the edge of the wood and the path continuing across some rough pasture. The end of the wood ended in a patch of long grass. Taking cover he squatted on his haunches and took a long look around.

He narrowed his eyes against the brightness of the sun, adjusting from the dark shadows inside the woods. Below him, to the right, he could see the stream. It flowed towards him from a small outcrop of rock, the head of a small V shaped valley, about three hundred yards away. Further up the valley he thought he could see some movement so he shifted position slightly. Now he could make out a line of small tents. He realised he was looking at a small camp well hidden and fully sheltered from the weather. At the far end of the valley Marmaduke could see some horses grazing peacefully, and beyond them there was a cart. He wasn't sure from this distance, but he would have sworn that the cart held two large wooden crates and some small barrels.

Suddenly a figure appeared at the top of the valley and waved a hand. He froze, for a horrible moment he thought he had been seen. Then he realised the figure of the archer from the beach had appeared below him in the gully and was walking beside the stream towards the camp. A second figure rose on the top of the hill above the valley and signalled. So, they have lookouts he thought, and congratulated himself on his caution. The archer had now reached the head of the valley where he was met by another three men. They talked earnestly for a while but no matter how hard he strained they were too far away for Marmaduke to hear anything that was being said. Eventually the archer continued up into the valley and disappeared behind a tent. Marmaduke considered his situation. He was convinced that getting any nearer would prove to be too dangerous. He hadn't seen the guards and had no idea how many men were in the camp. There were six that he knew of but there were enough tents for three or even four times that number. He needed to get back and tell Agnes what he had seen. If they needed to take a closer look he was sure she would be able to conjure up something a lot safer – even if was that misty, seeping thing. Without turning and moving very carefully, he crawled backwards into the woods until he was sure he was out of sight of the camp. Then he stood. He decided the best thing to do was to retrace his steps back through the woods to the waterfall and then up to the cliff top path and back to Cloughton. He was sure he could get some sort of lift in some sort of cart. If not he would walk.

As he passed through the woodland he congratulated himself that he had found the smugglers camp, then he stopped his congratulations. It suddenly dawned on him that the men in the camp weren't smugglers. The smugglers were lying dead on the beach. So who were the men in the camp and what were they doing with two crates of rifles and gunpowder?

He was almost back at the waterfall when he heard the sound of a twig snap behind him. He spun around just in time to see a figure rushing towards him, raising a large dagger, that was about to plunge into his back. He quickly dropped to one knee as the attacker, caught unawares, continued with his swung. The blow missed, the dagger making a vicious arc in the air above Marmaduke's head. Suddenly Marmaduke sprang back up, both of his hands raised in front of him. His eyes suddenly changed into two black, oval slits. His mouth split into a grin the revealed a set of very sharp pointed teeth.

The look on the attackers face suddenly changed. The expression of surprise as his blow missed turned to a look of horror as two hands came up towards his face. For a second he was sure that the hands suddenly seemed to be covered in fur, and sprouted vicious looking claws. Behind the claws was a set of fangs aiming straight for his face.

Marmaduke gave out a low growl as he raked his claws down the attackers face. The attacker screamed with pain and fell to his knees, his hands holding his torn and ragged cheeks. Blood spurted out from between his fingers.

Marmaduke stood with his hands dripping blood. He noticed a second man, a few yards behind the first. He was immobile, frozen in horror standing behind his fallen friend. Marmaduke growled again and sprang towards him. The man turned and fled back into the wood. Marmaduke knew that he would run back to the camp to fetch the others. Then it suddenly dawned on him that the others were probably on their way here already. It had been a very loud and piercing scream.

With one leap he turned and ran towards the waterfall. He reached its top, jumped down into the splash pool and ran across the beach towards the boat. He ignored the bodies laying there and ran towards the rear of the boat where a loose rope dangled towards the beach. Somehow it had come free from the rock to which it had been tied. He grabbed the rope and began tugging and pulling, dragging the boat across the rocks and the shingle, all the while keeping an eye on the waterfall. He reached the edge of the sea and continued dragging the boat until the water came up to his waist. Then he turned, pulled hard and clambered aboard. Beneath him he could feel the boat had caught the tug of the tide and was being pulled out to sea. Not quickly enough though. He rummaged around at the bottom of the boat and found an oar. He stood up and used it to push the boat further away from the shore.

Suddenly a number of figures appeared on top of the waterfall. Most of them jumped onto the beach, but one stayed where it was. Marmaduke recognised the archer, he was drawing his bow. Immediately Marmaduke threw himself into the bottom of the boat, pressing his body as flat as he could. He heard a thump and saw an arrow seemingly appear from nowhere quivering in the deck beside him. He rolled himself into a tight ball, looked around and saw the ships sail. He grabbed it and dragged it towards him trying to get his legs under cover. Sailcloth was tough, but whether it would stop an arrow was anyone's guess. He found out as a second arrow skidded off its surface and flew out of the boat.

Beneath him he could feel the swell of the sea and the movement of the boat as the tide took him further from the beach. He risked a look over the edge of the gunwale. A few of the figures stood knee deep in the water, looking after him, pointing and shouting, one even picked up a stone and threw it in his direction. It fell short. A couple more men ran along the path up through the woods. He could see them appearing and disappearing among the trees as they ran up towards the cliff top path. On the waterfall the archer released another arrow. It fell short, flashing through the water under his boat. He was out of range. He sat and watched the men as they gave up any idea of a chase and moved away from the beach. The archer stood watching him until he too suddenly turned and walked away. Even the men on the cliff tops stopped, realising that the boat would travel quicker than they could run. They gave up the chase and disappeared from view. He never noticed that high in the sky above him an eagle spiralled in the air currents turning into a small dot before disappearing out of sight.

As much as Marmaduke hated the water he realised the only way to get back home quickly and safely was by sail. Due to the steepness of the cliffs there wasn't really another option. As he reached the open sea a light breeze sprang up and, after much struggling and false hopes, Marmaduke managed to erect the mast and hoist what passed for a sail. It wasn't right, he knew that, but it would do. At least it caught the wind and powered the little boat towards safety. As he sailed towards safety Marmaduke sat with his back to the stern and took a knife out of his belt. Very carefully he began to scrape out flesh and blood from under his fingernails.

He had sailed halfway across the North Bay when Marmaduke realised that sailing into the harbour probably wasn't one of his better ideas. For one thing it would draw attention to himself and for another he wasn't sure whether he could steer the thing into the harbour without hitting something and drawing even more attention to himself. He decided the best thing to do was to run the boat aground before he got to the harbour wall. He scanned the shore line and came to the conclusion that he would beach it on the rocks, directly under the headland. There was no doubt it would soon be found, but let the locals make of it what they may.

Despite knowing the stories of shipwrecks and of ships coming to grief on rocks Marmaduke was surprised how difficult it was to run the boat aground. Every time he managed to steer the boat near to the rocks the undertow of the tide dragged it away again. Eventually with much effort and splashing of the oars, he managed to get its prow jammed between two rocks long enough to jump ashore. Leaving the boat behind he scrambled up the rocks onto the small path that ran around the headland and made his way towards the harbour and home.

As he walked into the house Agnes had a cup of tea poured out ready and waiting. There was a large brandy next to it. He drank the brandy off in one. She refilled the glass.

"How much did you see?" he asked wiping his mouth with the back of his hand.

"I picked you up as you were coming back through the woods, just before you were attacked." She replied calmly

"You saw that?" he replied.

She smiled, "Who do you think snapped the twig that made you turn around? Someone had to attract your attention!"

He paused and nodded a silent thank you. He sipped his tea. "So who do you think they are – I mean they don't look like your normal smugglers. Anyway I have a feeling that the normal smugglers are dead on the beach."

Agnes shook her head. "Not anymore, they took the bodies away with them. Probably worried they would wash away on the tide and end up here in one of the bays."

"That's careful of them, but it still doesn't tell us who they are."

Agnes poured a cup of tea out for herself. "I've an idea but I'm not sure. I tried to get near to their camp, but something's stopping me."

Marmaduke raised an eyebrow in surprise. "Stopping you, how?"

A look of annoyance crossed Agnes face. "They're shielding it. Oh I can feel something, I can sense something, but there's a blockage, some sort of screening that's preventing me from getting near enough to find out anything about them."

Without thinking Marmaduke flashed out his tongue and licked the bottom of the glass. "So how much did you see?"

Agnes gave him one of her disapproving looks. "Not a lot – once I found the blockage I tried to move around it. It's like there's an invisible bubble all around the camp. Then I picked you up walking through the woods. I saw you leave but someone in the camp knew you were there. I saw some men go after you – to finish you off. They're taking their secrecy very seriously – they don't want anyone to know they're there."

"You saw the fight?" As if remembering, Marmaduke began to pick at his finger nails.

"I saw you rip someone's face off if that's what you mean, yes, but once I saw you were in charge I drifted down to the beach."

Marmaduke looked puzzled.

Agnes sighed, "Well he screamed so loud I figured that the rest of the camp would come running and someone had to get down there and loosen the ropes on the boat, to make sure it wasn't tied up!"

He smiled "Ah, I was wondering about that. I must admit it did seem a bit….shall I say fortunate?"

Agnes ignored his comment, still thinking about the beach. "It was odd because when they appeared on the waterfall one of them seemed like an indistinct shape, a shadow, like he wasn't real."

"They were very real to me. Which one was cloaked?" Marmaduke said quietly.

"He was standing next to the archer. I could see the rest of them as clear as a bell."

Marmaduke shook his head "I don't understand. As far as I could see there was only the archer standing on top of the waterfall. All the others were jumping around on the beach."

Agnes tried to smile, but it wasn't a smile that was exactly laced with humour. "Neither do I."

The pair of them fell into a heavy silence.

Eventually Marmaduke remembered about the boat. This time Agnes's smile held a hint of humour. "Oh come on, you know that lot down at the harbour. Someone will have found it by now. I'll take a walk down and find out what they're talking about. I'll pick up some fish while I'm there. Cod or Mackerel?"

Marmaduke gave a little wince. "Anything but red meat!"

"That's why I suggested fish!" she said as the door closed behind her. Marmaduke shrugged, put his arms on the table, his head on his arms and slipped into a doze. He'd had enough excitement for one morning.

Chapter Four

When Agnes arrived at the harbour there was a small crowd of local fishermen gathered on the side of the pier. Below them, tied up against the outer harbour wall, a small boat bobbed about in the water. She walked among them. It always surprised Agnes as to how invisible a small elderly woman could be, even without magic. To be old was almost as effective as one of her cloaking spells. She moved through the fishermen picking up snatches of their conversation. "I tell you, it's not from round here!"

"Could have drifted down from Whitby way."

"No name on it!"

"No markings at all!"

"What sort of boat has no name?"
"Better keep an eye open for bodies!"

"Smugglers!"

"Probably washed overboard!"

"It wasn't rough this morning – wasn't rough yesterday either!"

"Perhaps they had an argument and fell out!"

"With each other or t'boat?"

"Both!"

The last comment raised a few grim laughs and Agnes drifted away down to a nearby fish stall. The boat was as big a mystery to them as it was to her. She hoped it would stay that way. At least the three men who had sailed in her and died on the beach were not locals.

Later that night, after a meal of steamed cod and potatoes garnished with fresh parsley, she sat in her front room. The lamp was low and Marmaduke lay sprawled across a chair. At first he seemed as if he was dozing, but closer inspection showed that his one good eye was open, watching Agnes very carefully.

She sat at the table. In front of her was a large pewter dish filled to the brim with water. Carefully she took a pinch of powder from a small tin container and sprinkled it over the dish. The water darkened and began to slightly fizz before a thin mist appeared, rising above the lip of the dish and spilling out over the table. With a sudden sweep of her arm Agnes cleared the mist and looked down into the pool.

A landscape appeared in front of her. Moonlight illuminated trees and bushes. A small valley appeared. She made another move and the valley grew larger. She was looking down directly into the camp. It appeared hazy, indistinct. She watched as shadowy figures moved around. She couldn't tell what they were doing. She could make out a glimmer of heat where a pot was boiling over a fire. At the far end of the camp, where the protective screening was weakest, she could make out the shape of horses tied up and a man brushing them down. She could also make out the shape of a cart holding two crates. Suddenly there was a ripple across the water and a face was staring back out, looking directly at her. Their eyes locked.

For a brief second Agnes was able to take in a pair of eyes staring down from above a large hooked nose. She could see black hair pulled back taught and a feather hanging down from the side of its face. Two white stripes were painted across the bridge of the nose and across a pair of high, thin cheekbones. The eyes seemed to be staring straight at her, penetrating. Suddenly the face let out a loud high-pitched scream. The water in the dish began to bubble before erupting, sending the displaced water to all corners of the room.

Marmaduke sprung to his feet. His knife appeared in his hand. Agnes sat back, dripping wet, her eyes were slightly glazed.

"They know someone's watching them!" Was all she said as she wiped the water from her dress.

Marmaduke slid the knife out of sight and made some tea. The two of them sat in silence for a while before Agnes opened her mouth. "They probably don't know where we are?"

"Probably?" he replied

"They're using something like a cloaking spell. Pretty basis stuff but… " she said before trailing off.

"Pardon my suspicious nature, is that a big "but" you are using there?" Marmaduke asked

Agnes thought deeply before slowly nodding her head. "Could be…If he has the talent there are ways he can trace us."

"Does he have the talent?"

Agnes shrugged. "I've no idea. We'd better assume he has. At least that way we won't get any unpleasant surprises!"

Marmaduke tried, but failed to hold back a grin. "Like a dish of water in the face?"

His attempt at humour was ignored. "Oh, a lot worse than a dish of water in the face. Whoever is out there has a power. I don't know how much power but it would be a grave mistake to underestimate it."

Marmaduke stopped grinning. "Who, or what is it?"

Agnes stroked her chin with her hand, Marmaduke didn't comment – it was almost the same movement he made to stroke his whiskers. "I'm not sure – but I have an idea, something about the dress and the face. I think he was the one standing by the archer. I do know that whoever it is they are a very long way from home. That just might work in our favour! I need to think for a while longer."

Marmaduke sprawled back in the chair again. "You mean to go off into your room and stare into space and do magic?"

"Yes!" She got up to leave but stopped as she reached the door. "Oh, by the way, I had a chat down the harbour. That boat didn't come from around here. Also there's no smuggling, no one's doing anything illegal at the moment. The Royal Navy's taken to patrolling out there."

Marmaduke raise an eyebrow.

"Convoy protection, seems there's a merchant fleet due in from the Baltic any time now." The door shut behind her. Marmaduke barely had time to curl up and shut his eye before it opened again.

"Forget something?" he said

"Only my brains!" she replied. "The convoy has something to do with whatever's happening. I know that, and I know an important event is about to happen – but … I think I need a chat with the garrison commander."

Marmaduke smiled "You think you can just march up there and demand an audience with him?"

Agnes's answer was simple. "Yes."

"But there's over two hundred men stationed up there."

Agnes shrugged "What's that got to do with the price of fish? Anyway there's actually more, but I only want to see one of them."

Marmaduke scratched his head. "Yes, but he is the main one."

Agnes smoothed down the front of her dress. "Of course. I only deal with the main man."

Marmaduke tried to be diplomatic. "But what makes you think he'll want to deal with you. There's layers of command between you and him. There will be papers to be filled in, questions asked. Getting through it all to see him will be like swimming through treacle. Especially for someone like…." He realised he was entering dangerous ground and tried to back off.

"Go on, say it!" Challenged Agnes, using her dangerous voice. Marmaduke inwardly winced. Agnes waited a few seconds, but Marmaduke knew better than to say anything else about the subject.

"Right!" She said, "If you're not going to say it I'll say it for you. Why would an officer and, presumably, a gentleman, want to meet an old crone like me?"

Marmaduke was very good at self-protection. He knew full well who opened the tins of cat food in this house.

"I didn't use the "c" word. I wasn't even thinking of the "c" word!" he protested.

"Well there's no need to worry your head about that. Leave that one to me!" She said as she turned and flounced out of the room. Marmaduke resisted an urge to lick behind his own ears.

The rest of the night passed uneventfully although Agnes slept fitfully. Images of the screaming face kept coming to her as soon as she shut her eyes. Despite her power she was glad that Marmaduke had taken to sleeping in a chair outside her room. The fact that he had two stout, loaded pistols lying across his lap was also a comfort.

The following morning Agnes slipped out of her house and began the steep walk up to the Castle gatehouse. Once she reached the top of the hill she stopped by the church to catch her breath and admire the view over the South Bay. She looked up and down the street and, when she was sure there was nobody about, she slipped behind the crumbling wall of a ruined monastery that had suffered from the attentions of both Henry VIII and the guns of the English Civil War. She was out of sight for a matter of seconds when there was a rustle of silk and suddenly out stepped a young, beautiful and elegantly dressed woman.

Agnes had certainly been very good looking in her younger years, but, despite her ability to slip in and out of the past and present, and her talent for warping both time and illusion, she still preferred herself in the skin and character of an old "wize" woman. It was a lot easier that way. That way she could avoid the constant battle to fight off male attention. The last thing she needed was a male partner, and Marmaduke didn't count because he was a cat.

However, occasionally she would slip back into her "flighty" character as the younger woman, mainly just to have some fun and recreation of the more risqué variety. In her eyes there was nothing wrong with leading men on, after all most of them deserved it, and it got her out of the house, she got to go out, have meals, drinks, and occasionally to the theatre or other entertainments. It did her good, got her out of herself and it amused her to create confusion among the male sex. This was the basis of her plan today. She rearranged her dress, pulled the front down a bit more, revealing a warm and inviting cleavage, and tottered off towards the Castle Gatehouse, occasionally dabbing her eye with a lace handkerchief.

As she approached the gatehouse the guards almost fell over themselves to help an attractive young damson very obviously in distress. They invited her into the gatehouse and offered her a choice of light refreshments before she had time to catch her breath. With much fluttering of her eyelashes and deep sighs that created havoc amongst her cleavage, Agnes managed to explain that she was the younger sister of the Garrison commander and that she had lost her purse on the way here and if someone could just run and tell him that she was here to see him, she would be very grateful. There was a very heated discussion between the guards as to who should go and who should stay to chaperone. Eventually an old and grizzled guard left the building and trudged towards the Garrison building.

As the remained of the guards fell over themselves to offer sherry, port, small beer and other things she didn't want Agnes sat in the middle of the guard room, dabbing her eyes and occasionally letting out a deep sob. Eventually the old guard returned bringing with him a young lieutenant who offered her his arm and gallantly escorted her from the gatehouse, across a grassy square and towards the building that housed the garrison. It wasn't a great distance but the walk took long enough for her presence to act like a very large stone thrown into their very small pool. The ripples she caused bounced off the castle walls. Suddenly soldiers of all ranks found a multitude of very good reasons to walk from the Garrison building to….well, to anywhere that led them in a direction that would pass the young woman.

She didn't need magic to feel the presence of many male eyes. Those unfortunate enough to be busily engaged on tasks that didn't involve a walk across the castle grounds stood where they were working. Some offered a slight salute, some doffed their caps, others made small polite bows.

She noticed a company of men had stopped cleaning out the barrel of a large cannon to watch her as she walked by. On the opposite side of the castle she could see another small group of men stop marching and lean on their rifles giving her the most appreciative of looks. One made a suggestive gesture with his hand and the others standing around him laughed. Agnes briefly considered arranging for the occupants of a nearby wasps nest to pay him a flying visit but instead simply pulled out a small fan and held it up to her face, more to prevent them from seeing her smile rather than to disguise her modesty.

She arrived at a building that she assumed held the commanders office and waited whilst the lieutenant knocked and entered. From inside the door she could hear a muffled conversation before the door opened and the lieutenant ushered her inside and up a flight of stairs. He knocked on a wooden door at the end of a short corridor. A voice asked them to enter.

She entered and found herself in a comfortable wooden panelled room at the corner of the building. Despite it being still September a fire blazed in the hearth. Large windows looked out over what she assumed was the parade ground. Through the windows she could see that army life was returning back to normal. Other equally large windows provided a view that took in both the North and South Bays.

A tall upright figure was standing looking out of one of the windows. As she stood the figure turned slowly around and she found herself facing a man in his late forties. He looked every inch the professional soldier. His uniform was smart, well tailored, and held an impressive amount of braid and medal ribbons. His face was adorned with a large moustache and a pair of accompanying, lamb-chop style, side whiskers that gave him the outward appearance of a startled badger.

As he opened his mouth to speak Agnes gave him one of her special looks. For the briefest of seconds the man's eyes glazed over, then cleared. Unless someone was looking very closely they wouldn't have seen a thing. Suddenly the commander stepped forward took both of Agnes hands into his and very politely kissed her on both cheeks. He offered Agnes a seat near to the fire and dismissed his lieutenant with a slight wave of his hand. The door shut behind him, leaving the two of them alone in the room.

The commander blinked. "I know you're not my sister for the very simple reason I don't have one. I have three brothers."

"I couldn't pass for a brother," replied Agnes, "I'm not even sure I pass as a sister." she added.

The commander opened his mouth. Agnes thought he was about to say something complimentary so in order to prevent further embarrassment or misunderstanding she moved her hand in a way that caused the words to die on the commanders lips and his mouth to drop open. Suddenly instead of the young attractive woman he found himself looking down at an elderly lady dressed head to foot in a very worn and unfashionable black dress.

Agnes opened her eyes very wide and held his gaze. "I'm here because I have to be and I'm going to tell you things because I have to. After you've listened to what I have to say we're going to talk. A situation has developed that calls for my intervention. It's both vexing and dangerous. I suggest you sit down and hear me out."

Without saying a word the commander walked across to a small table, reached out to a decanter and poured two glasses of sherry, one of which he offered to Agnes. She accepted politely and took a sip as he sat behind his desk. She put the glass down and started to describe the events of the last few days. He listened without interruption. When she had finished she leant back in her chair and moved her hand once. The commander blinked again.

 "Now do you understand?" she asked.

Silently he stood up and walked towards the window. For a few seconds he watched a group of soldiers march up and down in the parade ground.

He spoke without turning round "Before I say anything would you explain to me why I shouldn't call my lieutenant and have you arrested?"

"Common sense!" Agnes replied

Under his moustache the commander allowed a faint smile to cross his lips. "It has been said that common sense is a rare commodity when it comes under army regulations."

Agnes allowed herself a smile in return. She had his interest and they both knew it. "Are there any provisions in the army regulations about dealing with a wise woman? Especially one who comes to report a secret camp and the possibility of a plot that could endanger the garrison and the castle itself?"

The commander turned towards her, his smile had grown broader. "Ah, but madam, suppose I have no common sense?"

As the words left his lips Agnes simply disappeared. He blinked and looked around. He was alone in the room. He took a step forward.

"You might have trouble finding anyone to pin charges on." said a voice in his ear. He jumped and spun around. She was standing behind him.

As he spun around Agnes smiled again. "Now shall we both accept each others, shall we say professionalism?" she suggested.

The commander was a professional solider. He hadn't been promoted as a political favour or as a member of the gentry, he was a hardened soldier, and had got where he was by skill, determination and, despite army regulations, the use of good common sense. He nodded and led Agnes across the room to a table by the window. Then he reached down into a draw and pulled out a rolled up map.

"Show me where this camp is." he asked as he spread the map out in front of them.

She bent down and followed the coastline with her finger. "There, that's the waterfall." she said, allowing her finger to trace a route alongside the woodlands towards the camp. "That's it, there in that hollow."

The commander bent down and peered at the map.

"A good spot, easily defendable, I dare say you can see anyone approaching from here and here." The commander said examining the position.

"Could you attack it?" asked Agnes knowing what the answer would be. She wasn't disappointed.

The commander stood upright, stretched as if his back was giving him a slight twinge and began to pace across the room. "Oh yes I could, but it would be hard going. They'd see and hear us before we got anywhere near them. Then they'd just slide away into the woods. They'll have some sort of contingency plan. Fade away and regroup somewhere else. Then they'll harass us, try to pick us off one at a time. I've come across this style of fighting before, in the Americas."

Agnes raise her eyebrows, even her senses hadn't picked up on this possibility. "You've seen service in the colonies?" She asked.

He gave a small snort of derision "I have a feeling that it won't be the colonies for very much longer I'm afraid to say, but yes I did serve in America, in Boston actually."
There was something in his tone of voice that suggested to Agnes that things hadn't quiet gone as planned whilst he'd been there. "You don't have fond memories of Boston?" She asked.

He let out another snort of derision. "It wasn't one of my finest moments. I wonder, have you ever heard of an occurrence called the Incident on King Street? No, of course you haven't. It happened over nine years ago now, the 5th of March 1770 to be precise."

She shook her head, the date meant nothing to her. She made a mental note that he remembered both the year and the day. I bet he even knows what time it happened, she thought, but said nothing, allowing him to continue in his own time.

The commanders eyes were elsewhere now, they were back in Boston, reliving his memory. "It was probably one of the many sparks that helped to ignite the insurrection. Because the job of the army is to enforce legislation against the colonialists, good or bad, and there was more of the latter than the former, things had grown tense between them and us. One day a mob gathered and began to shout their protestations at a sentry. It was getting unpleasant and so some of his comrades came to help. They tried to move them on but the mob wouldn't back down and events spun out of control. Before anyone knew what was happening the situation escalated and soldiers lost their nerve. Some of them fired into the crowd. They said it was in self-defence but it still left three dead and a lot more wounded."

Agnes nodded in acknowledgement. "What happened next?"

He gave a sigh. "We got the men out and withdrew to Castle Island. There was an enquiry and arrests were made. Eight soldiers, one officer, and four civilians were charged with murder. At the subsequent trial six of the soldiers were acquitted, and the other two were convicted of manslaughter. They were given reduced sentences, they were branded on their hand. It wasn't a very popular outcome."

Agnes couldn't prevent her eyes from straying to the man's hands. There on the back of his left hand was a scar. At first she had dismissed it as evidence of an old wound, now she knew different.

"I take it you were that officer."

Again he sighed. "I wasn't near the place when it happened. But I was in command and I took my punishment along with my men. Shortly after that I got sent back home. The brand you see, it made us into targets, the army likes to think it looks after its own, it doesn't! I got shunted around various garrisons and eventually someone in charge thought I'd be out of the way up here."

There was a pause in the conversation as Agnes absorbed this new information. Eventually he broke the silence. "Can you describe them to me, in as much detail as possible?"

Agnes closed her eyes and recalled as many details as she could of Marmaduke's adventure. As she described the strangers the Commander slowly nodded.

When she had finished she opened her eyes. The Commander was now seated and his face was no longer smiling.

"So you think there's some truth in my story?"

He nodded gravely "I don't think. I know! Those men out there are either American troops or their sympathisers, maybe even a few French among them. As to the man with the bow, well he'll be an Indian scout. They are expert trackers and fighters, all sides have enlisted the natives over there. There's whole tribes fighting for us, for the French and for the colonists. I've known them sneak into camp and cut a man's throat before he wakes up."

Agnes nodded. It made sense. It all fell neatly into place. There was just one thing though she wanted to confirm.

"I'm assuming that you are aware of the reason that an enemy force is camping a few miles north of here?" She asked as innocently as she could.

The commander stood up and began pacing up and down again. "I might as well be frank. We have information that a small flotilla of ships is heading along the coast. They came down from Scotland and got far as the Humber. Now news comes from our garrison in Hull that says they've turned around and are heading back up the coast."

Agnes simply nodded. "Enemy ships?" she asked.

The commander gave her a long hard look. "How the hell do you....oh, yes sorry I was forgetting. Yes enemy ships, led by that American pirate John Paul Jones. He has four or five ships in his convoy and intelligence thinks they are going to try to attack the Baltic fleet. I estimate that they will meet right here – right under the guns of the castle. Before you say anything that's why I'm not going to order an attack on their camp. I just don't have enough men. I need to concentrate my force right here, just in case the Americans ignore the merchant fleet and try to land and attack the harbour like they did at Whitehaven."

Agnes knew this, she'd read up on her history but to keep up appearances she showed an element of surprise "Whitehaven?"

"Good God! The man's already caused havoc all over England, and Ireland, and Scotland for that matter. Since he left France he's been plundering and pillaging right through the Channel, the Bristol Channel and up into the Irish Sea. They attacked Whitehaven and Selkirk Castle in the Solway Firth. They made a landing at Whitehaven and tried to burn the place down, but they were foiled by the local militia. I've a feeling that's where your strangers got off his ship. They left the ship in Whitehaven and have walked across the country with a mission to blow the Castles guns up, leaving the Baltic Fleet exposed to their own ships. A neat little pre-arranged plan."

Agnes nodded in agreement "It's a plan alright, audacious…"

The commander interrupted her with a snort. "It appears that audacious is Captain Jones middle name. Word has it that he even tried to attack Edinburgh, but had to turn back. The tide was against him. Now he's sailing up and down the East Coast. Pretty soon we'll be able to stand on the battlements and wave at him as he sails past!"

Agnes looked out of the window. "That's all you will be able to do if you don't have any guns to fire. That's why they are planning on blowing up the castle walls – they hope to knock the cannon out, or at least make them unusable, and create as much confusion as possible!"

The commander nodded in agreement. "I'd already come to that conclusion. They've probably worked out that we've discovered the holes, but I shouldn't think that will stop them. They have their orders and I suspect that they are going to obey them as best they can. They'll do something to keep our minds and guns off Captain Jones."

The conversation came to another pause. They both looked out of the window. It was Agnes who asked the inevitable. "What are you going to do now?"

The commander thought for a moment before answering. "Well forewarned is forearmed. I'll double the guard for start, and I think I'll have someone take a telescope up the tower, just to see what we can see. Other than that I think we have two or three days grace. However once Captain Jones and the Merchant fleet appear on the horizon – well it's anyone's guess. Probably use the army's number one strategy."

"And that would be?"

"Point our guns at the enemy and keep firing at them until they go away. I find it's usually the best tactic." He smiled.

Agnes got up to leave. "Well it seems that you have everything in hand. I have done my job and I thank you for your time. It's been, shall we say illuminating."

The commander stood up and offered her his hand "No madam thank you. Without your knowledge, well, things could be very different." He stopped for a second, "Err, what you plan on doing?"
Agnes smiled "Oh I'll be around. I'll be keeping my eye on the situation, don't worry about that. There will be other visits from your younger sister."

The Commander nodded. "I didn't think for a moment that they wouldn't be!" he paused for a second then added "I suppose…"

Agnes smiled. "The same way I got in." she said.

"Allow me to escort you." The commander offered.

Agnes smiled. There was a bright shimmering sensation in the air that caused the commander to blink. When he opened his eyes the young lady was standing in front of him once again. She held a fan up to her face and fluttered her eyes at him.

"I say, that's dashed disconcerting you know." He said rubbing his eye with the back of his hand.

"Oh I know", replied the young lady fluttering her eyelashes, "I know!"

The Commander opened the door and led her out.

Chapter Five

That night, further up the coast, an owl skimmed over the lip of the waterfall and over the tops of the surrounding woods. It flew up to the edge of the wood and chose a high perch that looked directly onto the enemy camp.

Again all Agnes could see was a series of dim shapes moving around. Closing her eyes to help her concentration she allowed her senses to drift around the edges of the camp gently pushing and probing, trying to find a way inside its protective shield. She could make out the feint glow of half a dozen small campfires burning in the lea of the cliff. She found the Indian archer standing on top of the valley entrance. He had his bow held loosely in his hand and was gazing down the valley looking in the direction of the sea. She drifted along the edge of the camp to where she could make out the shape of the cart and two crates.

Suddenly she was startled by a sudden scream and a crashing in the branches above her head. Her senses snapped back to her. Automatically she threw herself backwards off her perch as viciously sharp talons

ripped through the space where, seconds ago, Agnes'
head had been. It was followed by a blinding
whirlwind of feathers.

The air shimmered. The world spun. Everything went
black.

Agnes opened her eyes. She could see the moon
through the branches of trees. Then she realised she
was lying on her back under the tree. Bracken had
broken her fall.

She closed her eyes again, took a deep breath, slowed
her breathing right down and sent a pulse of thought
through her body. She could wriggle her toes and
fingers. Nothing seemed to be broken, but she had
taken a few nasty knocks. There would be bruising.
She opened her eyes again and carefully tried to stand.
She made it on the third attempt and leaned back
against the tree. She let her senses seep out of her body
and very carefully let them drift through the trees and
out into the open ground beyond. She scanned the sky
above the wood, bracing herself for another onslaught
from the giant bird, but there was no sign of her
attacker.

Instead something else caught her attention. In the
distance she could hear a noise. It was the distant buzz

of conversation. Underneath the chatter she could also pick out a beat and the clink of glasses. Very carefully she let herself seep out of her body and across the fields. She could see lights, and as she got nearer she realised she was looking at a large public house.

Groups of people were mingling in a garden enclosed by a small hedge, containing a child's swing and a slide. People were drinking, a band was playing. She looked over a hedge and found a full car park. She pulled her mind back and sat down heavily. Interesting, somehow, as a panic reaction to the attack, she had catapulted herself forward into the 21st century. She had no idea how she had done it – she hoped it had happened through sheer survival instinct, but it worried her in case it wasn't. Agnes was the type of person that not only needed to know what was going on but also had to know the reason why. When she didn't know, she grew uncomfortable.

She pondered the possibility of returning home in the form of an owl, but instead took a few steps forward. The air shimmered and a seagull rose over the woodlands and slowly flapped it way through the evening sky back towards the town. When she got to the Castle she looked down on the ruins and allowed herself to be lifted by the drifts of wind that spiralled around the abandoned keep. The building she had stood in only a couple of hours ago was now ruined, not only missing the flight of stairs but missing its second floor entirely. Its walls were battered and worn with gaping holes in them.

She soared and swooped, allowing the air currents to lift and drop her over the cliff edge and down almost to the surface of the sea. With a flap of her wings she broke her freefall and flew across the town until she could see her own roof, only something wasn't right. There was a television aerial on her roof that wasn't hers. She landed on the chimney pot of the house across the road and watched her own front door. She didn't have to wait long. A figure appeared in the road below, it stopped outside her house, pulled out a key and let themselves in, closing the door behind them. That was her house alright, but it wasn't her time, this was a different time and place. It was a time and place where someone else lived in her house. This would take some working out. She flapped across the street and down the hill until she landed on the roof of the Three Mariners, only it wasn't a pub any more. She craned her neck to see into a downstairs room which once housed the familiar, dingy bar. Instead the room was brightly lit and an artist sat at an easel painting a landscape. She flew back to her roof. As she squatted on the chimney stack her attention was drawn by a movement out of the corner of her eye. She turned her head and saw an eagle circling high above the castles ruins.

Chapter Six

That night Marmaduke sat up, waiting in the kitchen.
By the time dawn had broken he was fast asleep, curled
up in a chair. As the early morning sunlight drifted
across the room he woke, stretched the stiffness from
his arms and legs and sniffed the air. There was still no
sign of Agnes. He was hungry and wandered into the
kitchen, only to find the remains of last night's meal.
This was not normal, what was normal was that if
Agnes knew she would be away for only a night there
would be food. This morning there wasn't, which
meant she had been delayed unexpectedly. This
worried Marmaduke, nothing unexpected ever
happened to Agnes.

He waited another hour, just in case. It came and went
and there was still no sign of the elderly lady so
Marmaduke decided the only thing to do was to go and
look for her. The last place she was headed was the
Castle, so it must be the first place to look. He
straightened his hat, adjusted his eye patch and combed
his whiskers. He made sure he had his knife hidden
inside his boot, and another hidden in his belt, around
the back where it wouldn't be seen. He slipped out of
the back yard and into a narrow back yard that led to

Castlegate. As he approached the Castle entrance he slowed down and moved carefully. Experience had taught him that people like him weren't always welcome. Sometimes people shot first and didn't even bother to ask questions afterwards. He was right, as soon as they saw him the two guards raised their pikes. Marmaduke looked at the vicious points on their top and stopped out of their range. He took his hat off and made a low bow.

"Good morning gentlemen. May I make an enquiry of your good selves?" he asked.

The two guards weren't used to being addressed as gentlemen. It confused them and gave Marmaduke an opportunity of asking his question before they saw him off.

"I am making enquiries concerning a woman…"

At the sound of the word "woman" one of the guards stopped being confused and gave a snigger. "This is a barracks. There's no women here. If you're looking for a woman try up in town. I hear the Beehive might cater for the likes of you."

Marmaduke gave a smile that exposed his two vicious fangs. Both guards took a step back and lowered their pikes.

"I think you might have misunderstood me gentlemen. I wasn't meaning any women. I was talking about a particular woman." As if to emphasise the point he carefully stroked the side of his head with his hand allowing the two guards a glimpse of his finger nails that appeared as vicious claws. The gesture wasn't lost on the guards. They had no idea who this man was but they instinctively knew they didn't want to get involved with him. They eyed the sharp end of their weapons and compared the distance between the points and the position of the man stood in front of them. They both seemed to be thinking the same thought. "There's two of us and he's at the end of our pikes." Before the thought could register long enough for them to do anything about it there was a shimmer in the air and a blur of what seemed like ginger fur flashed overhead. They looked at the end of their pikes. There was no one there. Instead they felt hot breath on the back of their necks and a voice in both their ears.

"There's a hard way and an easy way!"

They chose the easy way, dropped their pikes and turned around very slowly. Marmaduke stood there with his claws extended and very near to their faces.

"Now, if it's not too much trouble, could you please tell me if any women have come in and out of this gate in the last day?"

The guards looked at his claws, then his face, then his claws again. Suddenly they seemed very eager to talk, both at the same time.

"Both!"

"Yes, in and out."

"Yesterday."

"Left early evening."

"Late afternoon."

Marmaduke smiled. If it were only always this easy! "Can you describe her?"

They described her and added. "She wanted to see the Commander."

"Said she was his sister!"

Marmaduke smiled again. "And she left when…?"

"After about an hour."

"Yes, the Commander himself came to see her off."

Marmaduke nodded. It could only be Agnes. He smiled. When he spoke his voice came out a bit like a cross between a purr and a growl. "Thank you. That was the information I was seeking. I think you'll agree that was a lot easier wasn't it." He began to walk away, then suddenly turned, causing the two guards to jump back a step.

"Here's a thought to take with you, politeness costs nothing." He gave a low bow and walked away. As the two guards stood watching him go beads of sweat trickled down their faces.

"Better not mention anything." One said.

"Mention what?" replied the other.

They remained where they were, standing to attention. Marmaduke turned to the right from the gatehouse and made his way over the castle headland and sat at the top looking down into the North Bay. He needed to think. She had been here, she had found out what she needed to know and she'd gone again. The only question was where. It didn't need much thought, the only place she would go would be to have a look at the camp. He stood up and began to climb down the headland towards the shoreline below.

It was a long, but simple walk along the coastal path up to the cove and the waterfall. Throughout the trudge Marmaduke considered how Agnes must have travelled. She wouldn't have walked, she'd have travelled as a bird. A seagull was her favourite, sometimes an owl. She could have been and gone in the time it was taking him to walk, but she hadn't come back. She must still be out here somewhere, he looked around and resisted the urge to wave at a passing gull.

It took him the best part of two hours before he arrived on the top of the cliff looking down at the waterfall and the woodlands. He stopped, partly to catch his breath and partly to take in the view. Suddenly he became aware of movement on the path below him. The men from the camp were on the move. He quickly dropped into the bracken and crawled behind the trunk of a fallen tree. He froze. Now he could hear them. They walked in a quick, almost military manner, more relaxed than a march, but more determined than a ramble. He tilted his head as the wind caught their words and drifted passed him. He listened. They spoke quietly and breathlessly as men do when faced with walking uphill. He couldn't make out the words, but he was sensible enough not to try to move nearer, his senses told him that the men walking along the path were not walking with blindfolds on. They were alert and they were being led by the archer. By their sound of their footsteps he figured they must represent the entire camp. He had a feeling that if he went back to the little valley it would be empty. He waited until they passed by his hiding place, and then waited some more. Eventually he slid out from under the bracken and very carefully, and at a distance, followed them back towards the town.

After almost two hours they were almost at the North Bay when suddenly they diverted from the main path and took a smaller, hardly used path down the cliffs. Marmaduke dropped to his all fours and crawled to a position on the top of the cliff. He could see them descending a winding little path that led to a small building at the very end of the bay. It was a small and very dowdy inn that seemed to cater for travellers on the coastal path. Judging by its décor, or lack of it, and the general run down nature of the building itself, Marmaduke figured that passing trade wasn't very good, if indeed it ever had been. He noticed that the inn backed onto a small stream that flowed into the head of the bay and out to sea. Where the sea met the fresh water a small boat sat leaning sideways on the shingle. He settled back into the tall grass and watched. As they got nearer to the building the archer seemed to take charge. He gave a number of signals and the men fanned out to encircle the small building. The archer then gave another series of hand gestures and they stopped and took up positions. The archer then drew his bow and aimed it at the door of the inn. He nodded and two of them quietly moved forward, opened the door and entered the building.

Nothing happened for a full five minutes, then one of the men reappeared at the back door and gave a wave, which must have been the signal for the others. The archer nodded, lowered his bow and, without a pause, they all entered into the building. Marmaduke stroked his whiskers. He knew the men weren't local, so why had they entered the inn? Looking at the exterior décor it certainly couldn't be to eat. No one would consider eating in such a place. Of course there was the obvious reason, they wanted a drink, but something told Marmaduke that it wasn't just the alcoholic refreshment these men were after.

He sat back and waited. Sure enough after a short space of time the back door opened and the archer reappeared. He stood outside the door, looked left and right then made another hand gesture towards the building. The group of men left the inn and walked down to the beach, heading across the bay towards the cliffs and the castle. The archer followed them looking right and left, making sure they weren't being followed. It was at moments like this Marmaduke wished he'd counted them all, in fact he wished he'd learnt to count but, being a cat most of the time, it didn't really matter. That was another advantage of being human, you not only had hands to open cans, you also had fingers to count with.

He knew not all of the men had left the building, but how many had actually stayed behind was a bit of a mystery, it could be three or it could be four. He slid down the hill and scrambled towards the back door. Using every bit of available cover he crept towards the rear of the building. When he reached its wall he stood up and, with his back hard up against the rough stone, skirted around until he came to a rear window. Carefully he leant forward and tried to look inside but years of smoke, dirt and grime made the window opaque. He squatted down on his haunches and listened. All he could hear was the sound of the seagulls and the song of a skylark rising in the air from the hillside he'd just vacated. Suddenly the back door opened and a figure emerged. The man took a few steps forward and began to fiddle with the front of his trousers. Marmaduke froze as the man relieved himself then, just when he was in mid flow, Marmaduke sprang up and in one smooth movement pulled out a small leather cosh from inside his jacket and delivered a blow to the back of the man's head. Apart from a dull thump of leather hitting skin and bone the stranger fell to the ground without making a sound. Without stopping to see if anyone had witnessed him, Marmaduke dragged the inert stranger back to the wall and around the corner where he left him unconscious and folded double. He slipped the cosh back inside his jacket. When it came to fighting he really didn't have any scruples, after all everyone knows that a cat never fights fair, it fights to win.

He stood in silence and listened, there was still no noise from inside the building but Marmaduke knew full well that sooner or later someone would come out to see what had happened to their companion, after all the call of nature doesn't take that long. He stood just by the doorway with his back to the wall and brought out the leather cosh once again. He didn't have to wait long. After a few minutes the door opened and a head stuck out looking to the left and right. Before the face could register surprise at seeing him Marmaduke brought the cosh down once again and the figure slumped to its knees. Unfortunately the man fell half in and half out of the door. Throwing caution to the wind Marmaduke pulled the door open and rushed inside, leaping over the prostrate man. The man standing inside the door took one look at the apparition in front of him and threw his sword to the floor. Marmaduke took this as a sign of surrender so the tap he gave him with the cosh was light, but heavy enough to render him senseless. Three down, hopefully that was all of them. He glanced to the right and left –he was inside a small and dingy bar room with a couple of rough tables and benches positioned around the walls. Some seats were drawn up around the ashes of last night's fire. He looked across the room to a series of rough planks nailed to a series of old barrels that must pass as a bar. Behind it were a series of barrels some tapped and others unopened. A slow drip of ale came from one of the spigots. Marmaduke noticed three black leather tankards left on the bar. It looked like they had been helping themselves. Behind the bar was a small door that led to what could have been described as a kitchen – again there was an unlit fire in a large hearth over which an empty spit and an empty cauldron hung suspended from an old chain. Everything that could be seen was old and shabby, the place had definitely seen better days. A door at the back of the kitchen opened onto a small flight of stairs leading to the upper floor. Marmaduke took the steps two at a time and found himself in a small corridor along which were four closed doors, two on either side. He walked down the corridor carefully opening each door in turn. Three of them seemed to be bedrooms, but only if you were very desperate for a night's sleep. Marmaduke kicked a pallet of straw and a terrified rat scurried out of the door. He resisted the urge to chase it and opened the fourth door. It was someone's living quarters, only it redefined the word "living". The musty smell seemed to come from the old clothes that were scattered across the room. A tumble down bed took up most of the room at the foot of which was a large chest.

Marmaduke examined it – it was locked and there was no sign of it being forced. Despite the state of the room Marmaduke came to the conclusion that the strangers hadn't tried to rob the place. Just as well, he thought as he returned downstairs. The three unconscious men were still lying where he left them. He returned to the kitchen where he found some old rope. He pulled and tested it – it would do. He tied each of the men by their hands and feet, and then for good measure tied them up to each other. Satisfied that no one could escape from the tangled he'd created he stood back, one of the men was beginning to come around. His head jerked upright and his eyes widened when he saw Marmaduke and realised his own situation. Marmaduke smiled and gave the man another gentle tap with his blackjack. The man gave a grunt and his head fell back onto his chest. The last thing Marmaduke needed was conversation. What he did need was a drink. He picked up one of the leather mugs and walked behind the bar. As he turned the spigot he noticed a trap door below him. It was locked from the outside by a metal bar that slid through two metals rings. Marmaduke pulled the metal bar and very careful lifted the trap door. He stepped back in surprise as he saw two eyes looking back out at him.

Chapter Seven

Agnes circled the Castle headland still in the shape of a
seagull. There were thousands of seabirds living on the
cliff face and Agnes felt there would be safety in
numbers. She perched on the small rocky outcrop and
scanned the horizon. The eagle was easy to find – it
was about half a mile away being mobbed by a mixture
of other birds, mainly gulls and crows. Agnes watched
as it spiralled and swooped, out-flying the other birds
trying to fly back in the direction of the stranger's
camp. She almost felt sorry for it.

She followed from a safe distance and then, as the
eagle approached the site where the camp should have
been, it suddenly veered towards the end of the North
Bay where a small white building perched at the edge
of a stream that flowed into the sea. Agnes knew the
building, it was an inn called Scalby Mills. She
watched as the eagle circled high above the inn out of
sight of the many tourists who sat eating and drinking
at tables underneath parasols, well parasols when the
sun shone, umbrellas when it rained. The eagle
suddenly swooped to the ground and seemed to land
behind the inn, in a small valley that funnelled a stream
towards the sea. Agnes flew overhead and swooped

down to join a flock of other gulls who were
squabbling over some tourist left-over's.

The seagull waddled behind some bushes and, making
sure she was out of sight, Agnes changed and walked
up the small hill. Sure enough there was a figure sat in
the long grass looking over the top of the hill down
towards the pub and the tourists. Silently Agnes
walked up behind it. As she approached she made a
slight movement with her hand. The air shimmered and
the world seemed to freeze. The man slowly turned
around. The first thing Agnes noticed were his eyes.
They were wide with deep dark pupils. Suddenly they
darted sideward. Agnes caught a slight movement out
of the corner of her eye. She allowed herself a quick
glance to her left and was just in time to see a small
snake slither towards her through the long grass. She
flicked out a finger and a small flame appeared over
the snake. There was a small flash and then no snake.
The man's eyes widened further. Suddenly the air was
full of the sound of beating drums. Agnes held his gaze
and stared right back at him. The sound grew as the
beat gained speed getting faster and faster, louder and
louder. It filled the space between them and made the
air vibrate. Agnes could feel the beat drawing her in.
She could feel her foot begin to tap as the rhythms
echoed inside her head. Suddenly she snapped her

fingers and the sound stopped so quickly that the silence seemed almost painful.

"Oh you're good. Very good!" She said, "But I'm better!"

The man simply stared back. Agnes tried again. "I know who you are…. And I know why you're here!" The man looked around him. "Where is here?" he asked.

Agnes smiled. "Ah, now that's a good one. By my reckoning we're about three miles from your camp," she nodded inland in the right direction. "A mile from yonder castle." She nodded in the other direction. "And about three hundred years out of your own time!" His eyes showed a flicker of alarm as she added. "Oh yes, and we're not in the same world we started off in!"

The figure continued to stare at her, Agnes stared back, taking in the hooked nose, the long hair and the two stripes of white paint across his nose and cheeks.

"You see," she continued, "I have the advantage. I know who you are and I know your mission. I know you're from the Americas and I know you're here to put the Castle guns out of commission so Captain Jones can attack the Merchant Fleet."

The man in front of her simply stared back.

"And I know that you understand what I'm saying so it's no use playing dumb. They speak the same language over in the Americas. If you didn't speak English they wouldn't have chosen you for this mission."

The man nodded his head. "You are a wise woman." It wasn't a question it was a statement.

Chapter Eight

As his eyes adjusted to the darkness of the cellar
Marmaduke noticed that the eyes were watching him
from the top of a large piece of cloth that had been tied
around the man's mouth to act as a gag. As he took in
the sight, the figure grunted and wriggled around. The
wriggling drew Marmaduke's attention to the fact that
the man was tied up and laying on the cellar floor. He
jumped down the few steps and released the gag. The
man coughed and spat.

"Have they gone?" he asked.

Marmaduke nodded "Who are you? He asked.

The figure quivered with rage. "Me, I'm the bloody
landlord that's who I am. I'll never live this down.
Tied up and locked in my own cellar!"

As Marmaduke bent down to untie the ropes he
studiously ignored the two barrels of French brandy
and a chest that looked suspiciously like it contained
tea stacked in the far corner. As the ropes fell off the
man stood and rubbed various parts of his body to get
the circulation working again.

"The buggers. There were about a dozen of them. They didn't come in all at once, oh no. Three of them came in at first – ordered drinks and sat at the end of the bar. Then another three came in, ordered their drinks and sat opposite them. As I was serving the second lot one of the others came up behind me and bashed me over the head. The next thing I know I woke up tied hand and foot in my own cellar. Bastards!" he spat again.

Marmaduke carefully wound up the pieces of cut rope. "Fancy getting your own back?" He asked.

"Too bloody right I do. How?" replied the landlord.

"There's three of them laying unconscious on your pub floor. If you fancy you could give me a hand dumping them down here." He replied.

For the first time since Marmaduke had found him he saw a smile cross the landlords face.

"Nothing would give me greater pleasure." He said as he climbed the stairs back into the public house.

For the next fifteen minutes Marmaduke stood back in admiration of the inn keepers enthusiasm and originality when it came to the use of knots and ropes.

Even he winced as, one after the other, the inn keeper dragged the inert bodies across his rough wooden floor and dropped them down the hole into the cellar with a vicious kick in the ribs to help them on their way.

Together they closed the trapdoor, fixed the bolt and just to make sure, dragged two full barrels across the floor and positioned them in the centre of the trapdoor.

"Let 'em try to get out of that!" said the landlord spitting in the direction of the trapdoor. "Fancy a drink?"

Without waiting for an answer he pulled out two leather tankards and filled them from a smaller barrel at the back of the bar.

"The better stuff!" he remarked and smacked his lips in anticipation before taking a deep drink, after which he belched and he wiped his mouth with his sleeve

"Now, I'd appreciate it if you could tell me who I've got down my cellar!"

Marmaduke saw no reason why he shouldn't tell the truth. "Mercenaries. I think they're planning on attacking the Castle."

The landlord nearly choked on his beer. After a deal of coughing and wiping of his mouth, again with his sleeve he looked across at Marmaduke. "Either it's them or it's you!" he said.

Marmaduke looked puzzled.

"That's mad!" added the landlord as an explanation. "Can't attack the Castle, its bloody impregnable! Not only that, there's a couple of hundred soldiers up there."

Marmaduke smiled. "No, they're not mad, they're been paid, and I think you mean impregnable."

"Aye that's the word – you know what I mean. Anyway, even if they are being paid what about all them soldiers? They'll shoot at you whether you're paid or not. They're not too fussy up there you know!"

"They're not planning to capture the Castle"

Marmaduke said.

"But I thought you said….."

"They're not planning on capturing the Castle, they just want to blow up the walls, just enough to dislodge or disturb the guns up there. They are relying on the fact that the guns won't be able to fire if they're pointing in the wrong direction."

The landlord stopped drinking, his arm poised halfway between the table and his mouth. "You mean… Bloody hell, you mean they're preparing for an invasion!"

Marmaduke was impressed at how the inn keepers brain went from A, smashed right through B and ended up at C.

"Maybe…!" He simply said.
The landlord began to rise to his feet. "We should do something."

Marmaduke waved his hand. "Sit down. Something's already being done. The Commander of the garrison knows. His troops are keeping an eye open."

"Pity they didn't look in my direction" said the landlord and gave the back of his head a gentle rub. "I've got a lump here the size of a duck egg." He paused. "Do you reckon they know that they're on their way there right now?"

Marmaduke stroked the bottom of his beard. "Now you mention it – probably not. The speed they set off they're probably at the bottom of the cliff by now."

"Why not send them a signal?" said the landlord.

Marmaduke stopped for a second to consider what the landlord had just said. He spoke carefully. "First of all they're not expecting a signal, therefore they won't be looking out for one and secondly its bright daylight outside."

The landlord shrugged. "We could use the mirror." As he spoke he spat on his sleeve and wiped the grimy inside of the window – a greasy hole appeared in the dirt. He peered outside "It's sunny enough!"

 Marmaduke raised an eyebrow. "I take it you've got a mirror handy?"

The landlord flashed him a look that bordered on scorn. "Yes, I've got a mirror. It's upstairs next to the window which coincidently, looks directly out onto the bay and the castle."

A penny tinkled as it dropped through Marmaduke's brain as he remembered the brandy in the cellar. "I take it you know how to signal."

The landlord stood up and headed towards the stairs. He opened the door and paused long enough to turn towards Marmaduke "Just let's just say that not everything that happens around here happens at night!"

Marmaduke said nothing but followed him upstairs. In the bedroom the landlord pulled the mirror in front of the window. The glass itself was good quality, and was held in an oaken wooden frame supported on two uprights that allowed it to turn. Once in position Marmaduke could see it pointed directly to the bay and beyond towards the Castle. The sun was still high in the sky and at the perfect angle to hit the mirrors bright highly polished surface. The landlord moved the mirror slightly making adjustments and then slowly tipped it backwards and forwards.

Marmaduke raised an eyebrow "Code?" he asked.

The landlord shook his head. "No, the military use a different code to us, but they'll see the flashing light and hopefully report it to someone bright enough to work out something's going on, who'll hopefully report it to someone in charge, who in turn might just be bright enough to investigate!"

There were a lot of hopefuls in that sentence Marmaduke thought, but never one to discourage enthusiasm, he said nothing. He tugged at his beard once again and watched as the series of short flashes flew from the window across the bay and on towards the Castle. At the back of his mind he wondered if anyone would see them, and if they did, would they understand their significance. He watched for a few more minutes before making his decision. He turned to the landlord.

"You carry on here – I'm going up to the Castle. Whatever you do don't stop."

The landlord turned to Marmaduke "What happens when the sun goes down?"
"It'll only take me half an hour to get up there. By nightfall we should have the situation under control."

"You mean you'll have the buggers under lock and key?"

Marmaduke nodded. "Hopefully. Then we'll send someone back for the guests in your cellar."

The landlord grinned. "Give 'em a good kicking from me!"

Chapter Nine

The Commander was looking sadly inside the china cup he was holding, wondering if was really possible to mistreat tea as badly as the contents of his cup had been mistreated. For some reason unknown to him the stuff looked like tea, it even smelt like tea, but it tasted like metal polish. He was sat in his private quarters at the top of the garrison. It was his favourite room as it commanded spectacular views of both the North and South Bays. He stood up, with the offending cup in hand, and walked towards the window looking out onto the North Bay.

As he reached out to the latch his eyes caught the sight of a series of flashes coming from the far end of the bay. He watched carefully as it flashed on and off. It was definitely a signal, but who it was from, and who it was intended for he didn't know. He walked across the room to where a telescope stood on a large wooden and brass tripod. He dragged it across the floor and positioned it in front of the North Bay window, then pointed it towards the direction of the flashes and focused. A small white building came into view. The flashes were coming from an upstairs window. He stood up. From what he could remember that building was a small inn at a place called Scalby Mills. That told him whoever was sending the signals was probably local. As he stooped to take another look through the telescope he noticed another movement on the beach. He stood up again. It appeared to be the figure of a running man. Curious he adjusted the telescope. Refocused it showed a tall man with ginger hair, an eye patch and goatee beard, but the strangest thing of all was the way the man was running. It seemed as if he was loping. His stride seemed to be longer than normal and his body arched and flexed with every move. As he continued looking through the telescope the image of the man seemed to blur, move out of focus and for a brief second the figure changed from that of a running man to that of a very large cat. Instinctively he moved his head up from the telescope and check the scene with his own eyes. All he could see was the figure of a man running along the beach. The Commander shook his head and, remembering why he was at the window in the first place, opened it up, threw the liquid pretending to be tea out, shut it once again and quickly marched to the door. He threw it open and shouted down a flight of stairs. A soldiers head appeared at the bottom.

"Get the duty office up here, and quickly!" he ordered before striding back to look out of his window.

Across the bay again, the light was still flashing. The running man was getting nearer. There was a sharp knock and the door behind him opened. He turned to see a smartly dressed Lieutenant standing to attention on front of him.

"Smalls Sir, Lieutenant Smalls!" The figure announced.

The Commander nodded for the lieutenant to follow him and they both walked towards his desk, where he pulled out the map of the garrison. He jabbed his finger at the marks that indicated the holes under the castle walls.

"Smalls, I want half a dozen men positioned here, here, here and here. Tell them they are to hide and take cover in the bushes. They must, and I emphasise this, they must be well hidden. Their orders are to arrest and capture anyone who they find on the Castle Banks – and I mean anyone."

The Lieutenant looked up from the map. "Does that include locals sir?"

"It includes anyone they find." The lieutenant nodded. The commander continued. "I also want a couple of small platoons at the bottom of the hill, say there and there!"

Again he jabbed at the map. "As soon as they hear anything from the men above they are to throw a cordon around the base of the cliff and climb upwards to the walls – again they are arrest anyone they come across, including locals" he added.

The lieutenant nodded. "May I ask why Sir?"

The commander stood up and straightened his back. "We are laying a trap. I think we can expect some unwelcome visitors. Oh, yes and whilst I think about it, could you position a couple of riflemen on the Castle walls, here looking out over the North Bay. Tell them I'll be along in a little while."

The lieutenant nodded and began to walk towards the door. As his hand reached out for the door handle the Commander spoke once again. "Just one more thing, could you mention to the battery sergeant that I would like the guns to be moved so they all face the sea directly from the headland, and tell him to have all gun crews on stand-bye." The lieutenant paused. The Commander smiled at him. "I think some of our visitors may be arriving by sea!"

As the door closed behind the departing soldier the Commander quickly put on his uniform jacket, took his pistol, checked it was loaded and primed, pushed it into his belt and followed him out of the room.

Chapter Ten

Agnes made a movement with her hand. The air shimmered. The Indian watched with interest.

"Just so we don't get disturbed. A small cloaking spell. It assures us some privacy. I don't think it would help matters if the people living here suddenly discovered an Indian Shaman and an old witch sitting on their doorstep."

The Indian nodded and made a gesture of his own. Agnes braced herself against any magic, but the Indian dropped to his haunches and sat down. Agnes realise he was inviting her to do the same. She sat, although she declined to sit in the cross-legged position he had taken up. At her age her legs just wouldn't do it. She settled herself down and chose to speak first.

"Like I said I know who you are – A Native American – probably from the Tuscaroras, part if the Iroquois Nation if I'm not mistaken. Which makes it odd because most of your Nation are fighting on the British side."

The Indian smiled. "You are indeed wise. I bow to your detailed knowledge. I will not ask how it was gained. Many tribes make up our Nation, and many have different opinions and different points of view. As for myself, it is simple. I do not trust the British. So I fight for Mr Washington and the freedom of the Colonies."

Agnes nodded her head. "I know they all think that you're a tribal Shaman, but does anyone know how powerful you really are?" She could see from a slight movement in of eyes that her question had surprised the Indian. He did his best not to show it.

"You are good, white witch, very good indeed. No, no one even suspects my power. As long as I track and shield they never ask questions. They suspect I can shape shift, but they are mercenaries. They like their thinking to be done for them."

Agnes held his gaze. "What about back home?"

Again not a flicker of emotion crossed the Indian's face. "The elders of my tribe suspect. Only my teacher knows. It was he who taught me to fly as an eagle, he who showed me the secrets of becoming."

"He must have been a very powerful man." Agnes was impressed.

The Indian lowered his head. "He was, and his father before him."

"How were you chosen?"

The Indian looked up and straight into Agnes eyes. As he spoke she could feel the power that lay behind them. "The choosing was never in question. I was taught by my father."

Agnes nodded. Power through the generations, the most powerful magic passed down from father to son. Each time the power was passed down it grew stronger. She remembered her own grandfather and allowed herself a secret smile. The only thing he had passed down through her generations was a lack of money and an aptitude for drink.

As the Indian spoke he moved his hands and a long thin tube appeared out of nowhere. Agnes noticed the carving and colouring embossed along its stem that continued around the small bowl at the end. It was still smoking.

She nodded towards it in acknowledgement. "Is that...?"

He cut her off. "Many think it a pipe of peace. It isn't. It is just a pipe. By itself it has no power, it is what we put inside the pipe that contains the real power."

Agnes sniffed the acrid smoke. The smell seemed familiar. "I'm not sure smoking that is going to prove very productive." She said.

The Indian smiled. "For you maybe not – but for me… It helps to focus mental energy. Anyway it is not what you think. It is similar, very similar, but much more powerful. The herb you are thinking of would only create an impression that you are flying, with my herb you really are."

For once Agnes wasn't sure what to do. Seeing her indecision the Indian smiled. "I know, we have a problem." Agnes was about to speak but the Indian held up his hand. "Not one of culture, nor of the war. Oh we are involved, but only on the periphery. We allow ourselves to get involved as much as we need, we watch the affairs of men with amusement and a little bit of charity, but the problem I speak of is much greater. Our problem is that we are where, even the likes of us, should never be. We are in a future that for us does not exist – and we need to work together to find a way back – and that will take great bravery and our combined knowledge and skill – I cannot do it by myself. I need the help that can be gained through the use of herbs and, of course yourself!"

Agnes smiled and reached out her hand. The Indian passed her the pipe. Agnes carefully wiped the mouth-piece, put it to her lips and drew in the smoke.

Chapter Eleven

Marmaduke followed the invaders. He could just make them out in the distance, they were a least half a mile away and by the time he reached the base of the cliff they had disappeared from view. He looked up towards the Castle walls towering above the rocks and the bushes. Then he looked around. There was a path that forked a little way ahead of him. One arm led towards the sea and followed the line of the headland around the corner, until it reached the Harbour and South Bay. It was along there that the body of Sammy Storr had been found and where he had ditched the boat. A second track went up the hill leading to the right and wound its way up until it formed a pathway under the great stone arch that supported the road leading to the castle gatehouse. Marmaduke stood still and sniffed the air, then he dropped onto his all fours and sniffed the ground. Sure enough there was the trace of fresh scent. People had been here and they had taken the left hand path, up under the archway. There was a sudden noise and an arrow appeared embedded in the ground beside him.

Marmaduke leapt to one side, rolled and looked up. By the angle that it had stuck in the ground he figured it must have come from under the archway. They had left the archer to act as rearguard.

He looked up trying to make out where the man was hiding but the sun was beginning to disappear behind the castle, creating long dark shadows across the side of the hill. The best part of the day had gone and dusk was beginning to fall. The archer could be anywhere and by now the rest of his party would have had time to reach the holes, they were probably unpacking the gunpowder as he lay here. Without looking right or left he crouched down onto all fours and started straight up the steep hill making the most of the cover provided by the ferns and gorse. It didn't take long. When he reached the wall of the Castle he looked up and along the medieval stonework. Sure enough there were enough natural handholds to be found among the chipped and weathered stone to make it climbable. He checked the angle of the wall with the pathway lading under the arch. He hoped he was out of sight of the archer and began to pull himself up the wall. It was easy climbing and he soon found himself in a gap between the castellations. He threw an arm over, hauled himself up the final couple of feet, and dropped over the side onto a stone parapet that formed a walkway around the inside of the castle wall. As he landed on all fours he heard the sound of a very loud and very close click. He looked up to find himself looking down the barrel of a large and primed pistol. A voice spoke.

"Good afternoon, I'm the Garrison Commander. Thank you for dropping in. You're under arrest. Please, don't try to resist or I'll be forced to shoot you. Now very carefully stand up and start walking towards that staircase over there."

Marmaduke looked behind the speaker to see two troopers armed with rifles that were also pointed in his direction. He always made a point of not arguing with a loaded gun so he put his hands halfway up and began walking in the direction indicated by the rifle barrels. He was marched along the wall, down the staircase and across the parade ground. A smile crossed his lips when he saw that the garrison was a hive of activity. Soldiers were hurrying about in all directions, coming and going with an urgency that could only be described as military. Obviously someone had seen the signal and decided to act on it. Before he could see anymore he was ushered through a door, up a staircase, down a corridor and into a large spacious office. He stood whilst the commander ordered the guards to stand outside the door. Closing it behind them he then nodded to a chair opposite his desk. Marmaduke sat. The commander went straight to the point.

"I take it that you're behind the signals from Scalby!"

Marmaduke nodded. "I thought you'd seen them when I saw all the activity!"

The Commander sat behind his desk and leant forward. Suddenly he let out a large sneeze. He apologised, blew his nose with a lace handkerchief and leant forward once again. "Who are you?" he asked quietly.

Marmaduke leant back in his chair and folded his legs. "Does the name Agnes mean anything to you?"

The Commander suddenly sneezed once more. He placed his hand in front of his face and stood up. Before he could say anything else he sneezed again. He walked to the window, opened it, and drew in a couple of deep breaths of fresh air. When he turned back Marmaduke notice his eyes were red and watering.

"Agnes, yes I know Agnes, a very, err....interesting woman." He sneezed once more and dabbed at his nose with the handkerchief again.

"She could get you something for that cold." Marmaduke

The commander ignored the offer. "You must be her bloody cat!" he remarked.

For a second Marmaduke was stunned into silence. In the many years they had been together no one had ever suspected, let alone stated the fact. He was still stumbling to find the right words when the man spoke again.

"I was watching you run on the beach. Funny, but when I looked at you through the telescope, for a second all I could see was a giant cat..."

Before Marmaduke could deny anything the commander let a slight smile cross his lips and added, "…and I'm allergic to cats, always have been. I only have to be in the same room as one and I break out into sneezing fits!"

As if to confirm his self diagnosis the Commander let out another large and violent sneeze. Its force made the chandelier tinkle.

Chapter Twelve

Agnes closed her eyes as the herb took full effect. She felt more alive than she ever had before. She opened her eyes to see the sunlight streaming over the grass, making it shimmer like verdant silk blowing gently in the breeze. A jewelled butterfly hopped from flower to flower and Agnes could feel the slight breeze created by its wings. For a second she considered becoming one, to experience the world from the mind of a colourful painted butterfly.

Suddenly she became aware of the Indian sitting in front of her. He was slowly shaking his head. Then he pointed up towards the sky. She followed his gaze and become aware of a blur and a great flapping. In front of her an eagle stretched its wings and took to the air. It took three beats from its wings before it caught a 9thermal draught and suddenly soared into the blue of the sky. Agnes watched as the shape became a small dot before disappearing entirely.

She sat watching the patch of sky considering whether or not to follow. Something told her to wait. She waited. She had never become an eagle before. In her part of the world the sight of an eagle would cause consternation in the local community. It would be unusual enough for someone to notice and curiosities would be aroused and that would never do. Bearing that in mind Agnes always preferred to become one with the more common birds found around the seaside town, various gulls, owls, pigeons, and once on a very special occasion, a Robin, but that was at Christmas and a part of a different story.

There was a sudden swoosh, a sense of brown and a flurry of feathers. The grass rustled and once again the Indian was seated in front of her.

As he emerged out of the eagle he opened his eyes. "Speed alone will not suffice". He said simply.

Agnes's reply was equally simple. "I never thought it would!"

The Indian raised an eyebrow. At last, thought Agnes, a reaction.

"It will take speed plus impact…" she explained

The Indian interrupted her. "Impact?"

"Impact," Agnes repeated. "Remember, you struck me!"

The Indian nodded, his eyes looked down. Agnes paused to see if he apologised, but he didn't. She carried on. "Speed, plus impact, plus the collision of whatever forces we were using at the time. Remember we were both using magic? Somehow the combination of all those elements has thrown us here. Tell me, when you recovered were you still in the form of an eagle?"

The Indian thought for a moment and then shook his head. "No I was as you see me now."

Agnes pursed her lips. "Mmm so was I."

The Indian paused whilst he thought through the problem, eventually he spoke. "Do you think that has any bearing on the matter?"

Agnes voiced her theory. "I'm not too sure – but I think we need to recreate the circumstances as near as damn it!"

The Indian looked puzzled "As near as dammit?"

"As near as possible." Agnes explained.

The Indian suddenly put his head to one side, his eyes

suddenly wide with a mixture of surprise and fear. He spoke with a desperate urgency. "Quickly, seek cover. There is something above us. It is not good."

Agnes didn't need telling twice. With an agility that surprised herself she rolled under the cover of the tree. The Indian wasn't far behind. They both looked up. Through the leaves they could make out a shape in the sky. At first it looked like a large bird but something about the shape and movement of its wings told her it was no type of bird she had ever seen before. She looked across to the Indian who responded by putting his index finger up to his lips. They drew themselves deeper into the undergrowth and remained silent.

Agnes tuned her senses. She could feel the presence of something evil. She drew them back, worried whether the thing above them could feel her probing. She looked across to the Indian who was making short movements with his fingers. Everything went very quiet.

After a few moments the Indian let out a great sigh. "It has passed over! It was not a great cloaking spell, but it was enough." A look of relief crossed his face.

Agnes struggled to get on her feet. "What was it?"

"It is something I hoped never to see again – it is the Machinitou."

Agnes thought for a few seconds before finally saying, "Never heard of it. What is a… a… whatever you called it?"

The Indian repeated the word. "Machinitou, a great evil. It is a mistake, a god that was created by accident by Chemanitou the Master of Life. It is very ancient in our lore. I have met the creature before, many, many years ago."

Agnes raised an eyebrow. "What happened?"

"There was a great struggle. I managed to trap and defeat it, but in the struggle it killed my father."

Agnes was surprised, She realised she must be underestimating the power of the creature. "Oh, I'm…"

The Indian cut her off before she floundered anymore. "No, do not say anything. What happened was foretold. For my father it was a good day to die."

Agnes scratched her head at this bit of native philosophy. "Is there ever a good day to die?"

The Indian smiled. "Not really – but it is said to comfort us in our passing! It is one of our beliefs."

"Along with that thing we've just seen?"

"Unfortunately that creature does not exist just in belief. That thing is very real. You saw it with your own eyes."

Agnes stretched her legs and arms. "Well it looks like we've two problems. First getting back to our rightful time and secondly what to do about that Machinitou creature."

The Indian shrugged his shoulders and rose to his feet. "As to our first problem, I have no idea. Indeed I am not even sure where here is!"

Agnes nodded in the direction of the sky "And as to our evil friend?"

The Indian shook his head. "I am greatly puzzled. I cannot understand what it is doing here."

"What happened when you defeated him the first time?" Agnes asked.

She saw a look of sorrow pass across the Indians face as he recalled past times.

"At first I battled using my powers. The creatures were stronger. My father offered his help and together we climbed the mountain of our forefathers. There at the top we prepared a great magic, five days and nights we spent in preparation. When the creature came we unleashed such power that had never been seen by my people before, but again it proved too little. It was then my father used a very powerful magic to call upon some mighty spirits, the spirits of our ancestors. We attempted to lure the creature into a canyon where we prepared a great trap. As I was preoccupied with the rituals surrounding this task the Machinitou struck."

His voice faltered and Agnes could see the pain of the memory on the Indians face. She waited whilst he controlled his emotions. When he continued to speak it was with a firm and determined voice.

"It proved too much for my father. He was old and his spirit weak. It fled his earthly body. However his sacrifice was not wasted. His diversion allowed me to spring the trap. The magic of my ancestors proved powerful and created a web that held Machinitou inside a thundercloud until the great Chemanitou himself intervened and banished him from our time and place."

"And he sent him here?"

The Indian looked puzzled. "I have no idea. Perhaps he is finding his own way back to our time. Perhaps like us, he has found himself here by accident."

Agnes was not convinced. "It's a bloody strange coincidence if you ask me. Could the creature have followed you?"

The Indian gave a slight shrug. "That is impossible."

"Why?" All her life Agnes had specialised in being the one to ask the difficult question. She found it saved a lot of time in the long-run. Most people found this disconcerting, the Indian never even noticed. Instead he gave great thought to the question before answering.

"After the death of my father I left my homelands. I travelled east and found myself among the lands of the colonists where I saw many crimes committed in the name of your King. Then one night, in a town called Boston I heard a man named George Washington speak. His words touched me and I joined his cause. That decision led me to many places. I have crossed the great ocean with Captain Jones. I visited France and experienced the wonders of Paris where Captain

Jones and Mr Benjamin Franklin held court, where the plans of a great invasion were laid."

Agnes nodded, she had read the history of the planned invasion when she researched the "event" history had foretold. She also knew why it had failed. She held her council and simply nodded.

"Despite their plans it proved to be a failure!" he fell silent.

"No one could foresee that the troops would fall ill!" Agnes said.

The Indian sighed. "If they had paid attention to the details it could have been prevented. However, believe me, ten thousand soldiers all suffering dysentery was not a pretty sight. Captain Jones was not happy with this turn of events, he is to say the very least a little headstrong and he insisted that he continue his mission, to harry and attack ships along the English coast. The plan to attack the guns of the Castle was hatched somewhere on the journey. Captain Jones knew of a large fleet that would offer him the chance of great prizes. We came ashore at Whitehaven, undercover of an attack on the port. The rest you know."

"And the Machinitou followed?"

The Indian shook his head. "I think that if the creature was following me he would have had many chances to find me. We found ourselves here by accident. I am not sure that even with its powers the Machinitou could find its way here on purpose."

The two fell into a silence. Agnes could hear the night falling all around them. In the distance a dog fox barked. An owl hooted. A small creature caused a rustle in the undergrowth. Eventually she broke their silence.

"Could it be that there is more than one of him? That the Machinitou you banished is not this one. This creature is a different one, one that actually belongs here in this parallel world?"

The Indian thought about this for a long while. So long that Agnes began to think he had fallen asleep. She was about to lean over and shake his shoulder when he spoke.

"That is a good thought. It makes no sense that such a creature should follow me. Perhaps you are right. Perhaps the creature is a different manifestation of the same evil, only one born into and living in this world."

"My only problem with that theory is how come it knows you?"

 The Indian gestured towards the sky with one of his hands. "Perhaps it is drawn to my power. Perhaps it does not know me but recognises my power and has come to seek what or who can wield such a power. Also it equally could be drawn to you and your power."

The last comment worried Agnes. She had never considered that possibility. "I see what you mean. It cannot be from your culture. We are in the future and in a different world."

"It is a sad fact that evil exists everywhere. Perhaps the Machinitou itself is just a manifestation of that evil – perhaps my Indian race has personified that evil into the shape of the Machinitou. Whatever its name in this world it is alert to our presence. It will hunt us until it finds us. We were lucky. The cloaking spell worked. But it won't work forever. Already its power fades."

What about Chemanitou. Is it possible that he too exists in this world?"

The Indian fell silent once again before speaking. "If Machinitou exists so must his maker. Something created what we see around us. It might known by the same name, but the world has the same balance. Where there is evil there must also be good. We will trust in Chemanitou!"

Agnes nodded before asked the unspoken question that had crossed both their minds. "Could you capture it again?"

The Indian shook his head sadly. "Alas, I do not have the correct circumstances."

"You don't have the magic?"

The Indian shook his head again. "No I do not have the landscape, before I was able to lure it into a canyon. The holding magic was cast across the canyon top, like a lid over a pot. The magic held him in the canyon until Chemanitou intervened."

Agnes's mind began to race. "So basically all you need is something like a large hole to draw him into."

The Indian laughed. "A canyon is more than a large hole, it contains rock, ancient rocks that are part of the land, which in turn becomes part of the magic, and I have not seen such a place since I crossed the great ocean."

Agnes' mind was working overtime. An idea had dawned and she wanted to pursue it. If things were as she thought, it could work. It had to it was the only idea they had.

"I have a place in mind. It may not be as large as a canyon but it is constructed of ancient stone, and it is big enough that the creature could be lured into it."

The Indians eyes gleamed with interest as Agnes outlined her idea.

Later that night an owl fluttered out from the boughs of a tree and flew up into the night sky. In the distance sounds of people enjoying themselves drifted across the fields. Clinking glasses and the drone of distant conversation mixed and merged with distinct sound of a musical beat. The owl flew over them and up, towards the ruined Castle where it perched on the very top of the ancient Keep. Before long it was joined by a large black shape that seemed to drop silently out of the sky. Together the two birds dropped to the bottom of the empty shell of the Keep where, after a flurry of feathers, they disappeared. In their place stood an old woman and a Red Indian shaman.

Chapter Thirteen

Between sneezes the Commander crossed the room and opened all the windows as wide as he could.

"Nothing personal of course." He said as he turned back into the room.

"Of course." replied Marmaduke.

The commander moved to the table in the centre of the room and began to explain his plans to Marmaduke by standing at the opposite side of the table and pointing at the outstretched map of the Castle.

"How long ago did you put your men into position?" Marmaduke asked as he listened to the arrangements.

The Commander stopped to think. "It was whilst you

were running across the beach, say about thirty or forty minutes ago."

Marmaduke nodded. "That was when you gave the order, but how long will it take to get the men together and get them into position?"

A look of realisation crossed the Commanders face. "Surely they must be in position by now."

Marmaduke shrugged his shoulders. "The men were at least thirty minutes ahead of me, maybe more. Let's say it took fifteen minutes as I waited outside the inn, another fifteen to tie them up and find the landlord. I have a bad feeling that they could already be in place."

The Commander sneezed again. "In which case my men will find them in the places I sent them."

Marmaduke raised his eyebrow. "Will that be before or after they've planted the gunpowder?"
The Commander let out a short curse. "Come on let's find out. I'm going onto the ramparts to see what I can see."

The two men left the office and marched across the courtyard towards the walls. As they were about to climb the stone staircase the air reverberated with a mighty blast. The world seemed to explode around them. Suddenly the sky was black and filled with smoke, dust and dirt. Earth and stones fell all around them. Some survival instinct made Marmaduke press tightly up against the wall. He put out an arm and dragged the Commander after him. He looked up to see they were protected from the falling rubble by a small ledge that held the walkway around the parapet. The Commander began to move towards the courtyard but Marmaduke pulled him back.

"How many holes were there?" He shouted above the din.

As if in answer three more explosions in quick succession rocked the Castle from further down the wall, a hundred yards away and beyond. Marmaduke put his hands over his head to protect himself from the flying debris. His ears were ringing but, in amongst the noise, he could hear the sounds of gun-fire, and men screaming.

He grabbed the arm of the Commander and leapt towards the steps leading up to the rampart. The two of them reached the top as the dust cleared. Looking along the wall the ramparts were severely damaged. All along the top of the wall were holes created by missing stones. Marmaduke looked over the top of the wall, down the hill, towards the town. Stones and dirt from the explosion had caused some damage to the houses below. A chimney stack was missing from one house, another house roof now featured a large hole. He could see people running through the streets. He could hear screaming and confusion. At the foot of the castle hill a small troop of soldiers in their red uniforms were pinned down in the undergrowth. They were firing their guns towards a large hole under the Castle wall almost directly below him. There was no doubt that this was where the first explosion had taken place. The earth was ripped apart and gaped so wide that the very foundations of the wall could be seen. Above the hole, in the wall itself were a number of large holes and damaged stones.

Marmaduke turned his head to the right and could see some movement among the undergrowth. He pointed and the Commander followed his direction. They could see a small group of men furtively making their way around the base of the castle wall onto the headland. He turned to the Commander.

"They are heading back towards the North Bay. Get some men down to cut them off." he shouted.

The Commander seemed to shake his head. Marmaduke realised the man was having trouble hearing him. His ears must still be ringing from the explosions. He looked around. Inside the Castle there was confusion. Soldiers were running around trying to pull injured colleagues from the rubble. A Sergeant Major had taken charge and was barking orders. Stretchers were being gathered and the injured being attended to. Towards the headland end of the wall he could see that the guns were still standing. The gun crews were busy pulling them further away from the damaged sections of wall.

The Commander's eyes were not damaged and he could see for himself what was happening, and quickly realised that the attackers were heading back towards the North Bay, exactly where he hadn't placed any guards. He raced down the staircase and across the courtyard jumping over injured men and rubble until he reached the Sergeant Major. From his gestures Marmaduke figured he was ordering troops towards the North Bay in the hope that they would be cut off. He began to run across the parapet to the part of the wall that towered over the headland. He knew that once the attackers had reached the headland they would be heading towards the North Bay and back towards the inn at Scalby Mills. He doubted that, given the shocked state of the troops, they would succeed in their mission. He was now at the headland end of the wall and looked over the parapet. A shot rang out and he felt the wind of a musket ball pass too close to his ear for comfort. He ducked and moved to a hole in the wall. As he peered down he saw that the attackers had attached a series of ropes to large stable rocks.

Two men lay in the undergrowth with their guns pointing up towards the top of the wall providing covering fire for their comrades who were busy shining down the ropes leading towards the rocks at the base of the cliff. Without thinking he ran along the parapet. As he ran the shape of his body changed. He came to the barrel of one of the repositioned guns, ran along it and leapt over the wall. As he fell towards the ground he hoped it was true that cats always landed on their feet.

Chapter Fourteen

Agnes and the Indian stood in the centre of the deserted Keep. Long grass had grown on what was once a stone floor. Small saplings were growing up against the walls. Large clusters of ivy hung down from the walls. Pigeons disturbed from their roosting places fluttered between the four walls.

"Will this place do?" She asked.

The Indian looked up and down at the ancient walls. "There are many entrances,"

Agnes pointed at the holes in the stonework. "Once upon a time they used to be windows."

The Indian nodded towards various dark areas around the ground floor. "There are doorways as well."

Agnes tried not to sound offended. The man had wanted a stone trap and as far as she could make out, this building fitted the bill. "I never said it would be perfect. The stones are old though."

The Indian walked up to a wall and gently ran his hand across the stone blocks. "It is old."

Agnes was in great danger of losing her patience. "Will it do? If it won't I'll have to start thinking and come up with something else!"

The Indian nodded. "It will do, but it will take much work. First all the entrances must be sealed."

"What with?"

"Indian magic. I will begin to prepare. It will take some hours."

"What do you need?"

The Indian looked around the ground. "I think everything I need is here."

As he spoke he began to pull up some saplings and strip their whippy stems of its leaves. She watched fascinated as he formed the stems into tight circles. Then from his pocket he produced a reel of what looked to Agnes, suspiciously like darning wool. He then scratched around on the ground until he found some pigeon feathers. As he began to thread the wool through the wooden circle and attaching the feathers Agnes recognised the thing he was crafting.

"We call them dream catchers." She said.

The Indian looked up, a frown crossed his face. "They are emblems of great magic power. Each member tribe of my nation has a special pattern that weaves a special magic. They are a tribal secret, how do you know about them?"
A grin crossed Agnes' face. "I'm afraid in three hundred years time they'll be on sale in every nick-knack shop in the country!"

The Indian looked up from his work. "I do not understand this word nick-knack!"

Agnes tried to explain. "It's a shop that sells souvenirs, decorations, ornaments, stuff like that."

The Indian returned to his work "Do those who purchase these dream catchers make magic with them?"

Agnes shook her head. "No they just hang them up in their bedrooms where they gather dust."

"They have great power if used right."

Agnes was about to make a comment when suddenly a shadow crossed the moon. Both of them looked anxiously up towards the night sky. They both felt a distant presence.

The Indian bent down and concentrated on his work. He spoke without looking up.
"As I do this may I suggest you take up a place at the top of the Keep to watch for the evil one. Make sure you are well hidden and please remember his magic is powerful."
.

The air shimmered and a seagull rose from the ground slowly spiralling up to the top of the keep. There was another shimmer and Agnes appeared sitting at the very top of the building. She had chosen a spot on a ledge, next to a large crumbling tower where a once a doorway led onto the roof. Now the only doorway remained, the stairs and parapet had disappeared a long time ago. She drew inside its shadow, and just to make sure, cast a cloaking spell. She looked down. Underneath her in deep shadow she could just make out the shape of the Indian. He had finished making his magic symbols and was going around, doorway to doorway fixing a small wooden circlet to top of them all.

Once he finished the ground floor, much to her surprise, he began to levitate. He just rose in the air stopping at each of the ruined window frames where he repeated his actions, carefully placing his magic creations at the top of each window frame.

It took over an hour before he was satisfied that every entrance and gap in the outer walls was now covered. He rose up the wall and sat next to her.

"Now we wait." He said.

 Dawn was appearing as a crack of light over the horizon.

Chapter Fifteen

In the confusion no one from the Castle noticed a cat leap from the top of the wall. None of the troops positioned below the Castle noticed that it landed between a gorse bush and a large patch of bracken. No one saw it as it got to its feet, licked its face and smoothed its ears with its paws and then set off at a slow lope around the base of the wall. When the cat approached the area above the headland it dropped to its stomach and crept carefully through a gorse bush to peer out at the opposite side.

Just below the cat one of the attackers was pointing his musket towards the top of the wall, his finger resting on the trigger waiting for a suitable target to appear. A few yards further along a second attacker was in the act of reloading. Between them two ropes were tied around a large, solid looking rock. The ropes were taught, someone was using them to climb down the cliff face. The cat crept silently through the bushes carefully avoiding the sharp spikes of the gorse, until he was behind the attacker, stalking him as if he were stalking a bird. The car squatted, tensed itself and sprang.

As the cat exploded like a coiled spring from its hiding place the air shimmered and the cat disappeared. Instead the figure of a very angry Marmaduke crashed into view. The attacker heard the noise too late. As he turned his face he met two large, paw-like hands that raked his face with its sharp claws ripping gouges down his cheeks. He dropped the gun and then dropped to his knees, his hands going up to his hold his ripped cheeks. As the blood flowed through his fingers he let out a piercing scream.

The sound drew the attention of the second gunner who turned and levelled his fully loaded musket at the newcomer. Marmaduke quickly calculated the distance between them and realised that it was too great for him to jump before the gunner could pull the trigger. As he saw the flash and a puff of black smoke appear from the end of the musket he dropped to his knees and braced himself, waiting for the shock and pain of the bullet as it hit. Nothing happened. Curious he raised his head just in time to see the man let go of the gun and fall backwards clutching his chest. A patch of red was already appearing beneath his hands. As he fell his feet slipped from under him and he tumbled backwards down the steep bank. Marmaduke watched as the figure disappeared over the edge of the cliff. It didn't register with him that it would land in the same place that the body of Sammy Storr had been found, however cats never really understand irony.

He turned back towards the Castle and looked up. The Commander was standing at the top of the wall reloading a musket. Their eyes met and Marmaduke nodded an acknowledgment. The Commander nodded back and began to point towards the North Bay. Marmaduke understood. He checked behind him. The only figure visible was the man laying moaning and holding his face. Marmaduke resisted kicking him over the edge. He figured someone would be around to pick him up sooner or later.

Carefully he made his way across to the two ropes. They were still taught. Out of sight below him there was someone holding on, climbing down to safety. Marmaduke pulled a large knife from his boot and began sawing through the first rope. After a few seconds it snapped and snaked its way over the edge. Marmaduke hoped the climber had taken a hard fall. He repeated the action with the second rope and got the same results. This time it was more satisfactory, he heard a short sharp scream from below. H smiled and carefully he made his way around the headland until he was in full view of the North Bay.

Looking back towards the Castle he could see activity all along the wall. He also noticed a number of troops carefully picking their way down the disused track that led from the garrison to the North Bay beach below. At least the Commander had sent help. As he quickly zigzagged his way down to the beach he did some calculations. From the original dozen attackers three were accounted for in the inn cellar at Scalby, another two were either dead or laying injured on the Castle banks. That left seven, including the two whose ropes he had cut. Certainly they could be captured with ease by the advancing troops, eventually but the enemy had the advantage of time. The last thing Marmaduke wanted was for them to get back to the inn and release their friends. That would make the numbers back up to ten. Anyway the landlord would be no match for seven desperate enemies. Marmaduke hoped he remained at his window and had seen what was coming towards him and had decided that discretion was called for and had left his inn.

Below him figures appeared from under the cliff. They were running on the wet sand revealed by the falling tide. Some were slower than the others, as they held a figure between them who had a damaged leg that trailed limply behind him. Probably as a result of falling down the cliff.

Marmaduke checked across to the troopers. They were still only halfway down the cliff and then faced a chase over dry sand, a much more difficult surface to run on then the firm wet sand the attackers were running on. It didn't take a mathematical genius to realise that the fleeing men would reach the inn before the soldiers. Marmaduke bounded down the rest of the slope and gave chase. Overhead he heard the sound of gun fire. He turned to see a line of troops firing from the parapet of the Castle wall. The bullets fell short – the range was far too long. He hoped that the soldiers would realise that before a bullet fell his way. In a few long strides he was at the base of the cliff and hit the sands running. Up ahead one of the fleeing men helping his injured comrade had noticed him and had stopped. Marmaduke's heart sank when he realised the figure was drawing a bow. It was the archer. He stood with his legs apart and took careful aim. He wasn't fast enough and Marmaduke ducked as the arrow flew safely over his head. The man stood still as another arrow appeared in his bow. Again he pulled the bow taught and took aim. Marmaduke looked around for cover. Out here on the sands there wasn't any. The archer steadied himself.

Suddenly the earth shook with a series of deafening explosions. Startled the archer mis-aimed and the arrow went soaring into the sky above Marmaduke's head. Everyone on the beach stopped running and turned to look back towards the Castle. A cloud of dark smoke was drifting upwards from the top of the walls. The Commander had fired the castles big guns.

The thought that firing the cannon at the fleeing attackers was a bit on the extreme side crossed Marmaduke's mind. He looked along the beach to see where the deadly cannon balls had landed only to see that the attackers were standing pointing and looking behind him, out to sea. Marmaduke turned and followed their gaze.

As evening began to fall over the North Sea creating deep shadows in the Castle cliff he could just make out a series of white sails appearing on the horizon. As he watched, more and more masts and sails appeared, all seemingly heading towards the cliff and the North Bay. He looked back at the castle and saw a number of signal flags flying from the Keep. He remembered what Agnes had told him and realised that the Baltic Fleet had arrived. The enemy couldn't be far behind.

Chapter Sixteen

Agnes opened her eyes with a start. Dark shadows were creeping over the landscape. She looked across towards the Indian. He was sat next to her, with his back against the castle wall. His eyes were open. He was smoking his pipe with his hand over the bowl making sure the glow from the smouldering herb didn't show. He looked across as Agnes shuffled around to make herself more comfortable and try to get the stiffness from her legs.

"Shouldn't sleep outside at my age" she said. The Indian said nothing but raised an eyebrow and offered her his pipe. She accepted.

"Any sign of anything? She asked as she took a hold of the pipe, warming her hands over the glowing embers.

The Indian shook his head and they sat in silence together.

"What happens if, and when, we get back?" She asked, blowing a column of smoke out of her mouth. He tilted his head as if asking an unspoken question.

Agnes shrugged her shoulders, "Well strictly speaking we are on the opposing sides of a war!"

The Indian smiled and spoke with a low voice. "I think that people like you and I are never on anyone's side. We act as we see fit and as events dictate."

Agnes handed him back the pipe. "You know what I mean!"

The Indian took the pipe and took a deep pull before answering. "I will go home."

Agnes raised an eyebrow. "You can fly over the ocean?"
The Indian shook his head. "No. I will get a lift on Captain Jones ship back to France and from there gain a passage back to America."

Agnes could feel the effect of the smoke taking pace, her aches and pains were slowly dissolving. She framed her next question very carefully. "What makes you think Captain Jones will return to France?"

The Indian smiled once again. "Captain Jones will win the battle and sail away. Like you, I know history. I know what the future holds for my country. I know that your King will lose his colony and that a new nation will emerge. I think it will be interesting to see the birth of a nation. I have faith in Mr Washington and his Continental Congress."

"What about your own nation?" Agnes asked quietly.

The smile slipped from the Indians face like a cloud crossing the sun. He looked down towards the ground. "Like I said, I know history. I know the fate that the future holds for my people and the Indian nation. The bloody chapters of Wounded Knee and Little Big Horn are yet to be written. The likes of you and I cannot change history so there is nothing I can do but attempt to make the transition as painless as possible."

In deference to the times to come and the people yet to be born whose lives would be lost Agnes also lowered her eyes. "One of the saddest realisations of having power is the recognition that in the end our power leads to nothing."

The Indian looked back up at Agnes "But we do what we can. We try to make the lives of others easier, and we guard our worlds from the greater evil such as the one we are about to face."

Agnes sighed "But we can never alter history, we never really affect the bigger picture."

The Indian stretched his back. "Fate dictates the nature of the painting, we just fill in some of the detail, adding small splashes of colour here and there. It is enough."

Agnes thought for a moment and then smiled "That's a very good analogy. I will remember that."

The Indian began to rise to his feet. "And I will remember you Agnes the Witch, but for now, I fear that our fate begins to draw closer."

Agnes looked out across the bay. The moon was hidden by clouds and the sea looked black and uninviting. The hairs on the back of her neck began to rise. Her senses began to work overtime. Something was approaching in the darkness. She looked across towards the Indian.

He nodded. "The time has come. You know what is to be done."

As Agnes nodded the Indian stepped off the wall and for a moment hovered in the air in front of her. "Make sure that your holding spell is good. We will not get a second chance."

She watched as he slowly dropped to the bottom of the keep and squatted down in its centre. There was a spark and a small fire began to glow. The flames caught the wind and began to grow, casting strange, leaping shadows among the old stones. A thin trail of smoke spiralled up the building and dispersed into the night sky above Agnes' head. She could still feel the presence of something, but it was in the distance. Then her skin began to prickle. She felt the hairs on the back of her neck bristle. Suddenly all her sense began to scream at once. It was a lot closer. She felt a gust of wind and a heard a rustle of what seemed like leather wings. She became aware that something had landed on top of the Castle Keep, opposite to where she was hiding.

Agnes blinked, trying to make out what it was that she was looking at, but it was like trying to work out the shape of a black cat in a dark cellar, blindfolded. She concentrated and could make out two red eyes, tiny almost piggy like. They were focused downwards. The creature was watching the Indian sitting next to his fire. Agnes didn't move, in fact she didn't even breathe. She hoped her cloaking spell was strong enough. Slowly and very carefully, the creature stretched out a talon and a crackle of light streamed out and flew downwards, landing on the ground behind the Indian. A shower of sparks flared up and bounced among the ruins. The Indian remained motionless. The creature watched for a few seconds and then repeated its actions. More sparks flew around the floor, surrounding the Indian. Still he didn't move. The creature shifted position slightly. Agnes was sure that it tilted its head, trying to see what effect it had created. Below her she could still make out the shape of the Indian among the dying sparks.

Suddenly the creature reared up on a pair of legs that Agnes could only describe as those resembling a shaved goat. As it reared its front legs clawed viciously at the air. It let out a deep-chested howl, its open jaws revealing a mouth that resembled a deep, bloody gash. It drew its lips further apart showing fangs. As it gained its full height the creature let go another bolt of light. This time the flash landed right on top of the Indian engulfing his body. Agnes blinked as fingers of lightening spread from his body, over the surrounding ground, and up the walls of the building. A sudden flash illuminated the night, seeming to turn the inside of the keep into negative. A column of white flame shot up out of the keep, rising into the night sky, turning day into night. The sudden darkness made Agnes's eyes hurt. She blinked and through the after images could just make out the image of the creature. It simply stepped off the wall and dropped onto the ground beneath, covering the place where the Indian had been sitting with its leather wings.

Agnes wasted no time, ignoring the blinding after-burn in her eyes she began to cast a holding spell then, before it could form, she cast another and another. She kept on frantically moving her fingers, weaving the spells in and out until a series of silver lines appeared like silver spider webs criss-crossing the space at the top of the Keep.

Below her the creature looked up. She didn't stop. There was a sudden roar and she saw a huge red mouth coming up towards her. Still her fingers didn't stop. The creature hit the silver strands. For a second Agnes thought they would burst. They didn't. Instead they acted like elastic. They absorbed the force and bulged until the outline of the creatures face could be seen straining against the magical webs. Then the elastic reached its limit and catapulted the creature back down into the depth of the Keep. Agnes continued casting the web.

"That is good strong magic Agnes the Witch." Said the Indian. Agnes didn't turn around. Instead she concentrating on her spell and her fingers continued moving in their dexterous weaving. Below her the creature sank back onto the floor of the Keep. She risked a quick glance at the Indian. He simply shook his head and she continued weaving spell after spell. She sensed that the Indian was also weaving his own type of magic. A silver line appeared running around the top of the building where her webs were fastened to the wall. It weaved in and out of the ancient stonework and seemed to act as a type of seal.

Below her she could still make out the black shape of the creature as it paced and prowled along the inside of the walls. Every so often it sent up tendrils of light that climbed upwards, snaking over the ancient stonework, seeking out any cracks and weaknesses. She could hear it crackle as its fingers spread across the empty windows and skeleton window frames. Flashes and sparks occurred where the tendrils came into contact with the Indians own magical seals.

The creature let out a low growl and the tendrils seemed to withdraw and return into its own body leaving only a thick impenetrable darkness below her.

Before she had time to react Agnes became aware of movement to her right. She risked another quick glimpse and was surprised to see the Indian step out from the safety of the stone ledge onto the surface of the magical webs and begin to walk across them. When he reached the centre he stopped, slowly raised his

hands to the air and looked up into the night sky.
Below her in the darkness the creature began to howl, a
loud bloody curdling sound that reverberated inside her
head. She could see the open mouth and realised with a
shudder that it was getting nearer. The creature was
rising up once again. She then became aware of
another sound, a rhythmic chanting that seemed to be a
combination of words and sounds. It was coming from
the Indian. As if answer, a long way away she could
hear the beating of a drum. High in the sky, directly
above the keep, grey clouds gathered seething and
boiling

The creature struck the centre of the web directly
underneath the Indian. The web bulged with the force
of the impact. The Indian didn't move. Agnes looked
closer and realised that he was hovering in the air, a
few feet above the centre of the bulge.

Agnes kept working her fingers faster and faster,
sending out strand after strand to hold and strengthen
the web. Above her the grey swirling clouds filled the
sky.
Behind the clouds Agnes became aware of a pale
yellow, pulsating light that was forcing its way
through. Out of nowhere a wind sprang up. She leant
back forcing herself against the stonework, protecting

herself from the wind that was getting stronger and stronger by the second.

The creature let out a great howl and Agnes could see a taloned claw begin tearing at the inside of the web. To her horror she saw the strands of the web begin to rip and tear. She forced her hands to work even faster. Silver strands poured out from her fingers and curled and twisted across the top of the web. She concentrated her mind to strengthen the spell and cover up the rips. With a second ear splitting howl the creature redoubled its efforts. Suddenly a hole appeared and the clawed hand pushed its way through the web seeking out and reaching for the Indian who simply rose higher in the air, hovering just out of reach.

Agnes widened her eyes, made a slight adjustment with her hand movements and a thin line of fire shot from her fingers down a strand of the web, hit the creatures hand and covered it in a burst of flame. There was another howl and the hand disappeared.

Suddenly above the keep the clouds parted and a bolt of lightning flashed earthwards. It hit the Indian and danced over his body before crashing into the well of the keep. For a second everything seemed to stop. There was a deep black silence. Then a blinding flash followed by a huge explosion and everything went black.

Chapter Seventeen

A second salvo of cannon fire echoed across the bay. Taking advantage of the confusion Marmaduke began to run towards the standing men. The archer let off another arrow before he joined his companions and turned and ran, leaving the injured man behind. Marmaduke swerved and the arrow flew over his head. Despite his greater speed he realised that they would reach the inn at Scalby before him. He was hoping the landlord had noticed the commotion when, up ahead, he saw someone emerge from the inn and begin, to run up the hill behind it. Marmaduke recognised the landlord and watched as he disappeared behind the long grass just as the armed men reached the inn. Four of them took positions outside whilst the other two entered looking for their comrades. Marmaduke came to a halt as he realised three of them were now pointing guns in his direction whilst the fourth, the archer was aiming his arrows along the beach in the direction of the oncoming platoon of troops. He let fly with a quick salvo barely pausing between each arrow. At a bellow from their sergeant the oncoming troops scattered as the deadly arrows began to rain down among them. One trooper took a hit and fell to his knees looking with surprise at the arrow that now pierced his shoulder. Rifle fire echoed across the bay as the troopers took aim at the archer.

Marmaduke dived to his right and kept running. Up ahead was the little valley created by a stream that ran onto the beach from behind the inn. The area around the mouth of the stream was littered with rocks that would offer some protection. As he ran towards them, scrambling across the sands, he noticed the small boat laying on its side. He remembered seeing it there before, and realised it was the fugitives only way of escape.

A bullet whizzed through the air towards him but the shot fell short. He was still out of range which, as far as Marmaduke was concerned, was a very good thing. He carried on running at an angle to the inn, keeping out of range until he reached the opposite side of the valley and began climbing up the hill. The men outside the inn watched him until he ducked out of sight. He heard the popping of their guns and lowered himself onto his all fours and scurried to the top of the hill. He carefully pushed the long grass aside and peered down at the inn. As he watched the door to the inn opened and a group of men emerged. Three of them were rubbing various parts of their anatomy, trying to get feeling back into their arms and legs. Marmaduke allowed himself a small smile, it didn't last long. Now they had rescued their companions there were too many for Marmaduke to consider attacking.

Before he could figure anything out a salvo of gun fire rang out and one of the men by the door dropped to the ground screaming and clutching his chest. The troops from the castle had caught up with the chase and had continued to spread out in an attempt to encircle the inn. Leaving their fallen friend the rest of the men leapt down into the valley and began to drag the boat towards the sea. The Indian remained at the side of the building, his hands a blur as he drew arrow after arrow, firing them in turn at the troopers. The troops returned fire, concentrating on the men pulling and pushing at the boat. Their aim was good, two more bodies fell to the beach. Marmaduke stayed where he was. The last thing he needed was the troops to mistake him for one of the attackers.

Then suddenly it was all over. The men on the beach realised that the troops had better guns, and that they were pinned down. The tide was still some way out and there was no way they could drag the boat to the water's edge. Slowly they all raised their hands in the air in the universal act of surrender. As the troops moved forward to take the men prisoner, Marmaduke made his way down into the valley and climbed up the other side, heading towards the inn. He had forgotten the archer. As he stepped forward the Indian stepped out from the side of the building. He had his bow in his hands. The string was pulled taught. Marmaduke could see the trembling of the Indians arm muscle as he carefully aimed the arrow. Without even thinking Marmaduke suddenly leapt into the air. His body appeared to shrink and the arrow fizzed past his head, forming a ridge in his ginger fur. The archers face barely had time to register his amazement before a ginger cat had landed across his face. It's vicious claws dug into the side of his head. He screamed, dropped the bow and raised his hands to his face. The cat leapt off and took refuge on the roof of the inn. The archer was still holding his bleeding face when the trooper came up behind him and hit him on the back of his head with the wooden stock of his musket.

The cat leapt off the back of the roof and turned the corner of the building towards the doorway. It was open so he walked in. There was no one inside the building to see the flash of ginger fur and a large man with an eye patch suddenly standing there. Marmaduke walked to the bar, he looked behind it and found trapdoor to the cellar. It was open. He peered down. With the exception of the contraband tucked away at the far end it was empty. He closed the door and pulled a barrel over it to hide it from the eyes of nosy troopers. He had a quick look upstairs, it was empty. He walked back downstairs, helped himself to a drink and sat by the door. It wasn't long before a Sergeant appeared at the door holding a pistol.

Marmaduke held up his hands to show he had no weapons. The last thing he needed was a jumpy trooper. "I take it you've rounded them all up?" he said.

The sergeant looked across to Marmaduke and levelled his pistol directly at his chest. He stared at him for a moment and then lowered his pistol.

"You're that friend of the Commander aren't you?"

"That would be me, yes." Answered Marmaduke.

The Sergeant tucked his pistol back into his belt and looked around the bar.

"Any chance of a quick one before we head back?"

Marmaduke nodded. "Help yourself. The landlord ran off as they approached."

The Sergeant moved behind the bar and drew himself a large tankard of ale. He gulped it down and refilled it before walking across to Marmaduke and sat in the seat opposite him. He scratched the back of his head. "I don't suppose you know anything about them other blokes that came out of here?"

Marmaduke shrugged.

The Sergeant took another drink and wiped his mouth with the sleeve of his tunic. "I don't suppose you know anything about a bloke out there with half his face missing either?"

Marmaduke said nothing.

The sergeant scratched his head. "Odd thing is, he's a bloody redskin. An Indian all the way from the America's. Last thing I expected over here. Saw my fill of them over there. Funny lot, can never tell what they're thinking."

He paused to take another deep gulp. He burped and continued speaking.

"Anyway we'll march 'em back to the Castle. The Commander will be wanting a word with 'em. He takes an exception to strangers sneaking around blowing up bits of his castle. He'll be surprised to see we've brought him an Indian. Reckon that'll bring back a few memories for him."

Marmaduke had to ask, after all cats are curious creatures, and the sergeant told him the tale of the Commanders American adventures. He finished his tale by pulling his own sleeve up and showing off a deep scar on the back of his hand.

"It took some doing getting that bloody brand off!" he looked up into Marmaduke's good eye and added.

"Yes I was with him over there."

Before Marmaduke could make any comment the sound of another salvo of big guns echoed around the bay. The sergeant finished his drink in one long gulp and put the tankard down on the table.

"Sounds like it's getting a bit busy up there just now. I suppose I'd better be heading back." He gave a little laugh.

"Not that I can do much about anything. I'm army me."

He nodded in the direction of the South Bay. "That's work for the Navy. Anyway the main action's across the bay down Filey way. There's three or four warships lining up to have a right go at each other. All our lot are doing is sending over a few shots just to remind everyone that we're here!"

He stood and began to walk out of the room. Marmaduke quickly drank up and put his tankard onto the table.

"Mind if I come along. I'd like to see what's going on."

The sergeant nodded his head. "Not up to me to stop you. I reckon you knowing the Commander is all the authority you need. Anyway you can help keep an eye on the prisoners." He turned and walked out into the daylight. Marmaduke followed behind.

As they walked back onto the beach Marmaduke could see that the survivors had been roped together in single file and were been marched across the beach. The archer was being tended to by a trooper who was busy applying some sort of salve on his damaged face. Along the beach the bodies of the dead attackers had been laid out in a neat row and propped up out of the reach of the rising tide. A single soldier stood guarding them and snapped to attention as they walked towards him.

"Rest easy Parkins." Shouted the sergeant. "You're not expecting an inspection. You're here to make sure the gulls don't get 'em before we can get a cart down here. A couple of hours at the most."

The trooper saluted and stood at ease. The sergeant turned and marched back towards the headland and the Castle, the captives straggling behind guarded by the troop of soldiers who, Marmaduke suspected, were just waiting for one of them to step out of line so they had a legitimate excuse for clubbing them with the ends of their muskets. Two other troopers helped the archer along by holding him under both arms and half dragging him across the sands. Out on the sands two more troopers were helping the man with the damaged leg by dragging him across the sands.

Their march back to the Castle was conducted in a silence that was only broken only by the sound of the cannon firing out to sea.

Chapter Eighteen

Agnes opened her eyes. She was lying on her back in the middle of a gorse bush. Around her was a jumble of stone blocks and bits of broken masonry. A cloud of grey gritty smoke and dust drifted across her vision. The nearby trees were bent, branches had been torn off. The surrounding landscape looked like the aftermath of an explosion in a stone quarry. She realised she was lying on the Castle Banks, behind the Gatehouse. She looked up towards the Castles ancient keep. A great gash ran down its face and she realised that half of its southern wall was missing.

She groaned, her entire body hurt. She flexed her arms and moved her fingers. Then she stretched her legs and wriggled her toes. Despite feeling as if every bone in her body was broken everything seemed to be working, with the exception of her hearing. It seemed muffled, all she could hear were dulled explosions and distant rumbles. Her first thought was that somehow the explosion had affected her hearing and she had some sort of tinnitus.

She tried to sit up and instantly regretted it. The movement made her feel sick. She took a deep breath

and wriggled and struggled until she could lean her
back against the trunk of a tree. She closed her eyes
and began to breathe deeply, hoping the aches and
pains would fade away. Then she heard a grunt.
Painfully she turned her head. She saw the Indian
laying under the bottom of the Castle wall in a position
what could only be described as extreme discomfort.
She could see his chest moving as he breathed so she
knew he was still alive. She allowed her mind to drift
across his body. Despite the crazy angle of his foot to
the rest of his body she was able to determine the fact
that it was only badly sprained. It was his arm that
caused her to worry. It was broken. There was also a
very nasty lump on the back of his head. She felt his
consciousness begin to slip back and she withdrew as
he returned to consciousness.

He wriggled and managed to right himself so he was
sitting on the ground with his back lent against the
trunk of the tree. He was holding his arm carefully,
concentrating on flexing his fingers and wincing with
the effort. From the angle of his head she thought he
had hurt his neck, but then realised he had simply
turned his head to listen better.

"You can hear it as well?" she asked.

The Indian nodded. "The sound of cannon."

He tilted his head once more. "It seems to be coming from the direction of the Bay."

He looked up at the Keep and took in the surrounding devastation. "It appears we've succeeded."

They helped each other to their feet and gingerly took a couple of steps away from the tree. The town and the South Bay stretched out below them. Despite the darkness the skyline was illuminated by flashes of light.

Agnes nodded towards the sea. "I'll be honest with you, I've no idea what just happened, but I think we're back in the right time and the right place. I have a feeling that your Captain Jones has arrived."

The Indian flexed his arm and gave a wince. He gingerly placed his foot on the ground and winced again. He sat back down. "I think the Machinitou has been defeated. Our magic held until Chemanitou intervened."

Agnes tried to piece together the sequence of events.

"So that cloud…."

The Indian completed her sentence. "….was Chemanitou!"

"You summoned him?"

The Indian shook his head. "You do not summon Chemanitou. You ask. If you are blessed he comes."

Agnes paused taking in the enormity of what the Indian had said. They had survived due to a god's whim and that realisation worried her. She didn't believe in gods, Indian or otherwise.

"What happened to that Machinitou thing?" she asked after a few moments of reflection.

"I think that Chemanitou has dealt with him."

"Does that mean he's banished him again?" she asked.

The Indian looked grave and shook his head. "I don't know. Perhaps this time it was a more final fate, I think, I hope, but who can tell? Chemanitou did what he did." He flexed his arm and winced once again

"Your arms broken!" Agnes said, stating the obvious.

The Indian tried to make himself more comfortable.

"I know, and also I fear my ankle is sprained."
Suddenly there was a pipe in his hand. It was lit.

Agnes raised an eyebrow. The Indian tried to smile but
it turned into another wince. "Healing herb. Very
powerful medicine, takes away pain." He took a puff of
the smoke and passed it to Agnes.

Agnes knew she could heal herself, she also knew her
herbs were back at home. She wondered whether she
could learn the Indians magic of conjuring herbs out of
thin air, it would certainly be useful. She accepted the
offered pipe and sucked in the healing smoke.
At first she felt light-headed then a warm glow passed
down the length of her body. It felt like a very gentle
but deep massage that soothed her very being. The
stiffness disappeared, as did her aches and bruises. As
she passed the pipe back she felt good. It was then she
noticed that the Indian had been flexing the fingers on
his broken arm. Surely not, she thought. She was
wrong.

The Indian felt along his broken forearm with his free
hand and found the damaged area. He gripped, gently
at first, then suddenly squeezed hard. There was a
slightly audible snapping sound. Aware of being

watched he looked up at Agnes. "I found the break. It is now fixed!"

Agnes looked surprised. "You've set it?

The Indian shook his head "I do not know what this "set" word means."

"It means that you've found the break and put the bones back in the right position so they can knit together."

The Indian looked thoughtful for a few seconds. "Yes, that is what I mean, it is fixed!"

He bent forward and began to rub at his ankle.

Agnes leaned back against the tree. She had trouble taking in the fact that the man in front of her had just healed his own broken arm. He was powerful. In fact she wondered if he himself realised just how powerful he really was.

"Is it healed now?" she asked, trying to sound as casual as possible.

The Indian smiled. "The ankle? Yes! My arm, not just yet, even my powers have their limits. However it is healing fine, another hour should see the bones knitted and my arm as new again."

They handed the pipe backwards and forwards for a few minutes taking deep draws of the healing properties. Agnes could feel the regeneration moving through her body. After a while she had to admit she had never felt better. Even the day-to-day aches and pains caused by old age and wear and tear were healing. She smiled as she passed the pipe back. "You really must give me the recipe."

As they sat they looked over the small town towards the sea. They could see the masts of the ships that lay sheltering in the bays under the castle headland. They could also see the flashes and felt the explosions from the Castle cannon as they fired over their heads, across the South Bay and out to sea.

At the far end of the bay they could see six ships manoeuvring in the wind, attempting to get within firing range of each other. Positioning themselves between the Baltic Fleet and its would be attackers were the two representatives of the Royal Navy, the warship "HMS Serapis" and a smaller ship named the "Countess of Scarborough". Sailing up from the south on a heading that would soon meet and engage them was a line of four ships led by a second large warship, this one flying a flag bearing a design of stars and stripes. It was "The Bon Homme Richard" under the command of Captain John Paul Jones. Behind it were two frigates "The Pallas" and "Alliance" and a smaller brig named "Vengeance". They were too far away for Agnes to read their names but she knew them from her research.

Agnes nodded to herself, everything was as it should be, all the players were now in place, the action that history would come to know as the Battle of Flamborough was about to begin. Agnes pulled her shawl around her shoulders and settled down to watch history unfold.
"We might as well have a front seat." She nodded her head in the direction of the South Bay. "Are you still meaning to leave on his ship?"

The Indian nodded. "When the time is right I will leave with Captain Jones."

Chapter Nineteen

Marmaduke had marched back to the Castle with the escorted prisoners and watched as they were ushered away towards the garrisons gaol. Questions would be asked later. Information would be gleaned and acted on. The Commander had made the decision that the captives would be treated as prisoners of war.

"Better than being arrested as spies." He stated

Marmaduke had asked why and the Commander had explained his reasoning behind his actions.

"If we arrested them as spies we'd either have to hang them or shoot them. Whatever the option, I would be bogged down with paperwork, military courts and superior officers for months. Deciding they are prisoners of war means they have to be taken away to be questioned by the appropriate military authorities. That way they leave here and become someone else's problem."

They left the prisoners to their fate and walked onto the battlements looking down at the forest of masts that now filled both the North and South bays. The masts belonged to a variety of merchant ships, all jockeying for position seeking the protection of the Castles guns. The Commander nodded and another salvo of cannon fired over the ships in the direction of the larger warships positioned at the far end of the bay.

"Well out of range, just to remind them we're here really!" The Commander remarked.

Marmaduke watched as the warships manoeuvred themselves into positions that would allow them to fire salvos of cannon into each other. He could just make out the shapes of men on the ships decks, some were working at the ropes whilst others were hanging onto the rigging firing pistols and muskets at figures in the rigging of the enemy ships. Every so often he saw a figure tumble and hit the deck below. They never got up.

The Commander gave another nod and a nearby cannon fired once again. Marmaduke gave his head a shake as his hearing returned. The shot fell well short of the warships.

There was another loud explosion this time from across the bay. Marmaduke could see the puffs black smoke appear from the side of one of the warships. He was too far away to see the actual cannonballs fly, but he saw the results. Ragged holes suddenly appeared in white sails. He saw the top of a forward mast suddenly topple over and catch in the rigging and sails below.

"Wouldn't like to be in the Navy." The Commander commented.

Marmaduke raised the eyebrow of his good eye. The Commander explained. "Too damn difficult to retreat, I can't swim!" he paused waiting for some reaction to his small joke. Marmaduke didn't respond, he hadn't heard. Instead he was fine-tuning his hearing to a low, distant sound. At first it seemed like a distant roar that came and went, disappearing behind the more distinct and nearer sound of cannon and gun-fire.

He turned his head left and right trying to make out where the sound was coming from. It seemed to be getting louder and changed into a growling scream. The Commander must have heard it because he turned his head to Marmaduke.

"What is that…?"

The rest of his words were cut off by the sound of a huge explosion. They both turned their heads towards the Castle Keep in time to see it engulfed in a violent flash of white flame. Then, as if in slow motion, the far wall simply blew away. Suddenly their view was obscured by clouds of black smoke and flying masonry. Marmaduke dived to the ground and pulled the Commander with him. They lay there as a shower of stone fell all around them. Marmaduke could hear shouts and screams from the troops below in the Castles grounds.

Gradually the smoke cleared away. From his position up on the Castle wall Marmaduke began to make out the shape of the troopers. Some were doubling up, coughing from the effect of the smoke and dust. Some were just standing stock-still, staring with horror at the semi demolished Keep. Nearer to the building he could see injured troops, some figures lay on the grass not moving. All around them the ground was covered in pieces of broken stonework.

A sergeant suddenly appeared from nowhere and began shouting orders. Men arrived carrying stretchers. Some of the injured began to shout for help. The ones who didn't shout looked beyond help, their twisted and torn bodies lay at awkward angles among the stones. He heard a groan behind him and turned to see the Commander sitting up with his back against the wall. He was bleeding from a large wound at the side of his head where a lump of stone had caught him. Marmaduke looked back at the interior of the Castle. It seemed the military mind had taken over. Below him more sergeants were shouting orders. Junior officers were supervising the evacuation of the area around the damaged Keep. Injured men were being treated. A group of troopers were carefully stepping through the broken stone and rubble searching for any survivors.

Marmaduke put his arm out and helped the Commander to his feet. "Are you alright?" he asked.

The Commander shook his head and shouted back. "Head ringing like a damn bell. Can't hear a bloody thing." Marmaduke took his weight and began to help him through the scene of devastation back to the Garrison and his office.
They stumbled along the parapet and down the steps, all the while climbing over piles of loose and broken masonry. Around them soldiers were rushing around on what Marmaduke assumed was operation clean-up. Behind him he heard the Castle's cannon send another salvo across the bay. A thought struck him. If the castles guns couldn't reach the warships out in the bay it stood to reason that the warships couldn't reach the castle. Anyway just before everything exploded he'd seen both the larger warships firing their guns at each other. So what had hit the Castle Keep?

They eventually reached the Garrison building. It had suffered in the blast, half the window glass had been blown away and the brickwork was damaged with deep cracks appearing along the wall that faced the keep. The door had disappeared, its frame hung drunkenly to one side so Marmaduke entered the building and took the commander up the stairs and back to his office where he sat the Commander down in his chair.

He spoke but the Commander shook his head so he shouted.

"I'll try to find the doctor!"

"Don't bother trying to find the doctor. I'll be fine." The Commander shouted back.

"That's a nasty bump you've got on the head. It needs seeing to." Marmaduke insisted.

"I've just got a bit of a bump on the head. I'll be fine." The Commander shouted back.

Marmaduke realised that a conversation like this could go on for days. Instead he found a bit of paper and scrawled the words "Off to find doctor!" and left the room before the Commander could say anything else.

As he left the office he heard the Commander shouting for his lieutenant.

He walked across the courtyard towards the devastated building where he found the doctor patching up a troopers arm. The force of the explosion had ripped off most of the trooper's jacket and his arm seemed to be hanging limply. Marmaduke waited until the doctor took a pause in his treatment.

"The Commanders up in his office. He's taken a hit to the head and he seems to have gone deaf!" he said as the doctor wiped his bloody hands.

"Is he bleeding profusely?" The doctor asked.

"No – I bandaged it up. It seems to have stopped."

"Tell him I'll be along when I can. There's a lot worse injuries here."

Marmaduke looked around him at the wounded. Some were laying on stretchers, others sitting around. Most of them carried visible cuts and bruises. Some of them carried burn marks to themselves and their uniforms. Some had blackened faces and scorched hair. All of them looked to be more urgent cases than the Commanders injuries. Marmaduke figured that the doctor would probably get around to visit him sometime in the following day. He looked around. There was nothing he could do, the army seemed to have everything under control. At the far, seaward end of the castle the gunners were still in position, taking it in turns to fire off more warning shots over the masts in the bay below. Around the base of the damaged keep work parties had been formed into chains of troopers who were removing broken masonry and large stones.

Now that the smoke and debris had cleared away it was obvious that the explosion had occurred halfway up the keeps tower. The top half of the west wall had completely disappeared taking with it sections of both the north and southern wall. For some reason the East wall, the wall that faced the sea, remained intact. He also noticed that all the debris had been blown away from the tower, a fact that indicated to him that the explosion had occurred inside the building. Something bad had happened. He might only be a cat but he knew well that the devastation could not have been caused by a cannonball aimed from the warships in the bay. For a start the west wall didn't face the sea. He felt a shiver pass up his spine as he walked around the building. He looked down. Among the jumble of broken stones he found a small twig. It had been cut and made into a circle. Bits of broken string were tied to it. Tied to the end of one of the bits of string was an eagle feather. He picked the device up and slipped it into his pouch. The hair on the back of his neck began to bristle. All his instincts told him that something strange had occurred here.

Two officers armed with notebooks had appeared and were looking up at the building and assessing the damage and risks of the remainder of the building tumbling down. They were pointing to a part of the building that seemed to be at the epicentre of the explosion. Marmaduke took a few steps towards them, where he could eavesdrop their conversation. They were, it seemed to him, blaming the explosion on a stray spark near a powder store. He gave a secret smile. He knew that once their report had been formalised the army would have their own satisfactory reason for the explosion.

He looked up towards the Garrisons upper floor. The Commander was standing there looking at the destruction below. Marmaduke could see he wore a bandage around his head. He was surrounded by officers who all seemed to be busy writing things down and passing them to the Commander. He smiled to himself. Despite his injuries the Commander was still in charge. As everything was under control Marmaduke walked to a deserted part of the Castle, a small alleyway near to the main gatehouse. Out of sight of everyone he seemed to disappear in a blur of ginger fur. A cat walked out at the other end of the ally and headed for the gate.

The Castle entrance was full of people. Most of them had climbed up from the town to get a better view of the sea battle still raging in the bay. Most of them had been protected from the blast by the Castle wall, but they had watched open mouthed as large pieces of stone flew above their heads. Some of the townsfolk, those coming up the hill and those at the edge of the crowd, had been hit by flying debris. Troopers were helping them inside the Castle where those that needed medical attention could receive it. Newcomers had rushed up to find out the cause of the explosion. Excitable voices and shouts and screams filled the air. In all the bustle and confusion, no one noticed a cat slip through the open gate and make its way along the edge of the Castle wall until it came to the headland. The cat sat quietly. One of its ears twitched. It could hear voices. It slunk under a gorse bush to get nearer.

Chapter Twenty

Out at sea the two warships were locked together in what seemed to be a slow dance of death. Both ships were ablaze. They had sailed close to each other, firing at almost point blank range as sailors threw grappling irons between the two ships. As they closed together their top masts and rigging had become entangled with each other. Sailors were desperately running up the rigging with axes, chopping at the tangled ropes and spars as each of the ships poured cannon fire into each other. On the decks both crews were engaged in vicious hand-to-hand fighting. Cutlasses and pistols flashed by the light of the flames. Agnes nudged the Indian and pointed towards "The Bon Homme Richard."

"Captain Jones ship appears to have been hit on the waterline. Look it's beginning to list."

The Indian nodded gravely.

They watched in silence as the other ships of the convoy began sailing around the two main combatants, firing recklessly into the melee. Two others had broken away and were engaging each other in an exchange of broadsides.

Suddenly there was a large explosion from inside the Serapis. A sailor from the American ship had run across the spars of the main mast and was dropping grenades onto the deck below him. One of them had hit a gunpowder store. The burning gunpowder, set off other charges nearby, and soon the rear half of HMS Serapis lower gun-deck was devastated the fires and explosions killing or severely burning many of the gunnery crewmen. Some leapt into the sea to extinguish their burning clothes. Five guns were now out of action.

Away from the two warships and moving with the wind away from the main fight, were *Pallas* and the *Countess of Scarborough*. *Alliance* was catching up fast, though, and as the near-undamaged, speedy, well-armed frigate approached, Agnes watched as the captain struck his colours. The ship had surrendered.

As night fell a number of signals passed between the two warships. Both of them were now badly damaged. Leaning against each other as the Alliance sailed around them seemingly firing at random.

"He's going to sink them both!" Agnes exclaimed.

The Indian nodded gravely. "My captain will have to abandon the ship soon."

As he spoke a number of men suddenly appeared on the deck of the American ship.

Agnes pointed to the decks. "He's released his prisoners."

Seeing he was now both damaged and outnumbered the captain of the British ship struck his colours and the Americans began to board his ship.

Agnes watched in silence as the guns stopped firing and a number of little boats bobbed between the two ruined warships evacuating both the survivors and the wounded. Soon small boats were bobbing all over the sea. Some of them instead of heading towards their respective ships, headed straight towards the coast and the beach.

"Deserters and escaped prisoners I should think." Remarked Agnes.

They beached in the bay where they were met by townspeople who helped them ashore and tended the injured. Some men, probably prisoners of the American simply slipped away in the night.

The Indian stood up. "It is over. It was a mighty battle. They will talk of their escape this day for many years to come."

Agnes smiled. "Captain Jones will return to America as a hero."

The Indian rose to his feet. "And I will return with him. Come Agnes the Witch. It is time to say goodbye. It is time I joined my countryman."

Agnes raised an eyebrow, she couldn't resist it. "You do know that Captain Jones isn't American, he's a Scotsman, from the land to the north of here." she added, just in case the Indian didn't know what a Scotsman was or where they came from.

The Indian smiled back. "By the time the news travels across the ocean Captain Jones will be one of the most famous Americans of all."

"And you?"

The Indian shook his head. "I will not be famous. Once this war has ended I will return to my people, to watch over them in the difficult years to come."

Agnes lowered her eyes. "I do not envy you."

The Indian shrugged. "It will be hard, but it is necessary. It is written!"

He paused for a few seconds. "Now in honour of you, your trust and your company I will take my leave."

The Indian took up one of Agnes' hands and gently brought it to his lips. As he kissed the back of her hand there was a sudden blur and a striking grey and white herring gull hovered in the air in front of her.

It caught an air current and swept up into the night sky. Agnes watched as it stretched its wings and rode the airs currents across the bay. She watched until she saw it land on the afterdeck of the American warship and disappear out of sight.

On the ground where the Indian had been sitting she saw a pipe and a small bag of herbs. She smiled to herself as she picked them up and put them into her pocket. There was a rustle in a bush behind her. She didn't turn around.

"You alright?" asked a voice behind her.

"I am, but you've been hiding in that bush so long you must have got cramp." She replied.

Marmaduke stepped forward and sat down beside her. "Just keeping an eye on things, making sure you're alright."

"Oh I'm alright. The Castle keep took a bit of a beating though." She added.

"I know. I was there when it exploded. There's a couple of fatalities and lot of injured men up there."

"There's more out there." she said nodding in the direction of the bay now illuminated by the burning warships.

"I dare say there will be a lot more before the war ends."

Marmaduke scratched the back of his ear with his hand. "And what war were you fighting?"

Agnes sighed. "The usual one, good against evil. Light against dark." She suddenly stood up. "Come on I'll tell you about it over a tin of sardines, without toast!"

Marmaduke let out a low purr.
The two of them carefully picked their way down the Castle embankments until they came to the road that led to her house. She paused at the end of her street as people hurried up and down carrying lanterns. She nodded to a couple of acquaintances. Salmon John walked by pushing a wheelbarrow full of loose stone. She raised an eyebrow.

"Might as well make the most of it – I could do with a new wall. Keep next doors bloody cat of my privy!"

Beside her Agnes felt Marmaduke bristle. She said nothing but smiled and walked on. As she entered her own street she noticed a group of people standing in front of her house looking up at her roof. They turned as she approached. She looked to see what they were looking at and noticed a large hole ripped in her grey slate roof. She could just make out the end of a large lump of stone sticking out of the broken slates against the night sky.

"That'll take a bit of fixing." A voice said.

Agnes looked up into the night sky "It'll wait till the morning, it's a fine night!"

She entered her house and went upstairs. As she surveyed her damaged bedroom Marmaduke began to rummage in his pouch and pulled out the Indian charm

"I found this among the rubble."

She took it and examined it closely. "I never did work out how he did that." She said, almost to herself.

"Is it important?"

"It was…it's not anymore. Once I've got this mess sorted out I'll hang it the ceiling just above my bed."

Marmaduke nodded and wandered downstairs in search of sardines.

END.

ABOUT THE AUTHOR

Graham Rhodes has over 40 years experience in writing scripts, plays, books, articles, and creative outlines. He has created concepts and scripts for broadcast television, audio-visual presentations, computer games, film & video productions, web sites, audio-tape, interactive laser-disc, CD-ROM, animations, conferences, multi-media presentations and theatres. He has created specialised scripts for major corporate clients such as Coca Cola, British Aerospace, British Rail, The Co-operative Bank, Bass, Yorkshire Water, York City Council, Provident Finance, Yorkshire Forward, among many others. His knowledge of history helped in the creation of heritage based programs seen in museums and visitor centres throughout the country. They include The Merseyside Museum, The Jorvik Viking Centre, The Scottish Museum of Antiquities, & The Bar Convent Museum of Church History.

He has written scripts for two broadcast television documentaries, a Yorkshire Television religious series and a Beatrix potter Documentary for Chameleon Films and has written three film scripts, The Rebel Buccaneer, William and Harold 1066, and Rescue (A story of the Whitby Lifeboat) all currently looking for an interested party.

His stage plays have performed in small venues and pubs throughout Yorkshire. "Rambling Boy" was staged at Newcastle's Live Theatre in 2003, starring Newcastle musician Martin Stephenson, whilst "Chasing the Hard-Backed, Black Beetle" won the best drama award at the Northern Stage of the All England Theatre Festival and was performed at the Ilkley Literature Festival. Other work has received staged readings at The West Yorkshire Playhouse, been short listed at the Drama Association of Wales, and at the Liverpool Lesbian and Gay Film Festival.

He also wrote dialogue and story lines for THQ, one of America's biggest games companies, for "X-Beyond the Frontier" and "Yager" both winners of European Game of the Year Awards, and wrote the dialogue for Alan Hanson's Football Game (Codemasters) and many others.

OTHER BOOKS BY GRAHAM RHODES

"Footprints in the Mud of Time, The Alternative Story of York"

"More Poems about Sex 'n Drugs & Rock 'n Roll & Some Other Stuff

"The Jazz Detective."

The Agnes the Witch Series

"A Witch, Her Cat and a Pirate."

"A Witch, Her Cat and the Ship Wreckers."

"A Witch, Her Cat and the Devil Dogs"

Photographic Books

"A Visual History of York." (Book of photographs)

"Leeds Visible History" (A Book of Photographs)

"Harbourside - Scarborough Harbour
(A book of photographs available via Blurb)

"Lost Bicycles
(A book of photographs of deserted and lost bicycles available via Blurb)

"Trains of The North Yorkshire Moors
(A Book of photographs of the engines of the NYMR
available via Blurb)

The York Sketch Book – A book of drawings of York.

Printed in Great Britain
by Amazon

40902721R00136